CINNAMON ROLL SECRETS

KATHLEEN SUZETTE

Sign up to receive my newsletter for updates on new releases and sales:

https://www.subscribepage.com/kathleen-suzette

Follow me on Facebook:

https://www.facebook.com/Kathleen-Suzette-Kate-Bell-authors-759206390932120

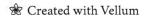 Created with Vellum

The alarm went off, and I'd like to say that I jumped out of bed with a spring in my step on this beautiful autumn day, but who am I kidding? I rolled out of bed and stumbled over the shoes I'd left on the floor the night before, barely managing to grab hold of the corner of the dresser to keep from doing an ungraceful nosedive and knocking a half-full bottle of water to the floor with a clatter. Thank goodness the lid was still on the bottle.

I glanced back over my shoulder. Alec was still sleeping, and my cat Dixie was curled up at the foot of the bed. He barely raised his head to regard my sleep-induced shuffle before stretching and returning to his slumber.

I shook my head, slipped my slippers onto my feet,

and padded down the stairs. It was my favorite time of year—Fall. Or autumn, for you fancy folks. The trees were beginning to turn brilliant shades of yellow, brown, orange, and burgundy, and all shades in between. It was still early in the season, so the beautiful foliage for which New England was famous had not yet fully unfurled. But give it time. In another month, our streets would be filled with the brilliant colors of fall.

I held onto the stair railing as I descended. It was just after 5:00 a.m., far too early to be out of bed, but I'd had cinnamon rolls on my mind for days. I'd been thinking about them so frequently that the cravings had built up, and there was no denying it now. I had to make some cinnamon rolls. There's something about the yeasty goodness combined with sweet cinnamon that is perfect for fall. Comfort food at its finest. Of course, it's perfect any time of year, but who doesn't love warm, sweet baked goods in the fall? And pumpkin spice lattes. We can't forget those.

I flipped on the kitchen light and headed straight for the coffeemaker. Without some caffeine, I wouldn't be able to stay awake long enough to make the cinnamon rolls. I hummed under my breath as I measured out the coffee into the machine. I normally made freshly ground coffee from whole beans, but I didn't want to wake Alec with the sound of the grinder. Even though he was asleep upstairs, sounds carried in this house, especially at this hour. Why does it seem that the earlier it is in the morning, the louder everything becomes?

I poured water into the machine and then went to my baking cupboard to get the ingredients for the cinnamon rolls. Alec had to go to work in a couple of hours, and later, my best friend Lucy and I would go for a morning run. I didn't know if I could hold off tasting a cinnamon roll until after the run, but I was going to try. Not that it wasn't a lost battle before it had even begun—it was. I love cinnamon rolls in case I haven't mentioned that before.

I set the ingredients on my kitchen counter and began working on the dough. Measuring out the yeast reminded me of the bread I used to bake for my first husband. He loved nothing more than freshly baked bread, and for a time, I made it several times a week. How had I gotten away from that? Alec would love some freshly baked bread now and again. I made a mental note to look up my recipes for bread so I could make some for him.

Next, I measured the flour and some sugar into the bowl, and the dough came together quickly. Perhaps I should have waited to do this on the weekend when Alec and I would have time to laze around in the morning and enjoy ourselves, but it was Wednesday, and I couldn't wait for the weekend.

Mentally, I was making plans for all the fun things I wanted to do this fall. I had a new grandbaby who had so many firsts to experience, and I wanted to be there to see them. Pumpkin patches, apple picking, baking, and we couldn't forget her first Halloween. Not that she could do much at seven months old, but we would do what we could, and take plenty of pictures so I could show them to her later. The adults in her life would have a ball at least.

My favorite part of making cinnamon rolls was kneading the dough. There was something about twisting and turning the dough over and over that I enjoyed. My mind wandered as I worked, and if I had had any stress, this would certainly help work it out. Who needed a stress ball when you had cinnamon roll dough to work with? I twisted and kneaded the dough for ten minutes before rolling it into a ball and placing it in a bowl that I'd buttered to prevent sticking.

The bowl of dough went into the oven to rise, and I headed to the living room to start a fire. I was inviting trouble by doing this because I planned to go out into the chilly morning air in a bit. It was going to be hard when it was nice and toasty inside, but I love a fire in the fireplace, and I wanted one this morning.

I looked at the picture of my granddaughter on the fireplace mantle and adjusted it. She was the most beautiful baby I'd ever seen. I didn't think I'd ever be able to say that about a child who wasn't my son or daughter, but believe me, when you have a grandchild, it changes everything.

With the fire started, I headed back to the kitchen to make the icing for the cinnamon rolls. I'd debated whether I wanted to make cream cheese frosting or a thinner icing to drizzle over the warm cinnamon rolls. I decided on the latter because it was more traditional in the house I grew up in. Or rather, it was more traditional for the cinnamon rolls that my grandma had made when I was young. She had taught me everything I knew about baking, and I was feeling nostalgic this morning. My mother, bless her heart, couldn't bake to save her life. But she could cook just about anything else better than anyone I knew, so I did the baking for her when we got together, and she did the cooking.

I sifted powdered sugar into a bowl and then poured in some vanilla extract and kneaded in some softened butter. I kept my butter in a butter bell, which kept it nice and soft for most of the year. Butter was one of my favorite ingredients and I kept it at the ready.

A bit of cream made the icing just the right consis-

5

tency. I covered it with plastic wrap and set it back on the counter.

I stretched and cracked my neck—something my mother hated me doing—and Dixie wandered into the kitchen and yowled at me.

I turned to him. "What are you doing up so early, mister?"

He meowed plaintively at me.

"All right." I refilled his bowl with food and rinsed out his water bowl, placing fresh water next to the food. He ate hungrily, and I washed my hands, made myself some coffee, and debated making Alec a travel mug to take with him to work. I decided I would wait until he got up. I hoped the cinnamon rolls would be ready for him so he could take one or two with him to work, but it was going to be pushing it for time.

I went to my kitchen window and looked out at the weather. It was still dark out, but the patio light showed the trees nearby were just beginning to lose a few leaves. It would be another month before they shed significant amounts. I inhaled, savoring the moment. If there was a way to extend this season, believe me, I would do it. Although I loved what came next—Christmas was a beautiful time of year—fall was always my favorite.

I took a sip of my coffee and decided to bring it upstairs to change into my running clothes and shoes while the dough finished rising. Treading back upstairs in the dark, I found my running clothes. Alec was sleeping peacefully, and I didn't want to wake him.

Once dressed, I hurried back downstairs for another sip of my coffee. Lucy and I planned to run on a path that led along the edge of town and through the woods today. I don't know why, but we didn't usually take that route, and I was looking forward to it. With all the trees turning colors, it would be a great route to take during the fall.

I took another sip of my cinnamon coffee and sighed. Cinnamon was one of my very favorite spices, and I was going to get my fill of it this fall. When the first rise was done, I rolled out the dough, spread the cinnamon mixture on it, then cut them and back they went into the oven for the second rise.

I went back into the living room and curled up in front of the fireplace with Dixie on my lap, resting my head back against the overstuffed chair. My cup of coffee was in my hand, and I took another sip, then closed my eyes, dreaming about my days as a little girl in Alabama. My grandmother had been gone for years now but my mother, sister, and brother still lived there. Not to mention all the people I'd grown up with. There was something about home that I could never extract from my heart, no matter how long I lived in Maine. But I knew that if I ever moved back to Alabama, leaving Maine behind would break my heart just as much as my longing for Alabama did now. After all, it was home, too.

"Allie, what are you doing?"

CHAPTER 2

I sat up with a start, still clutching my cup of coffee and almost sending Dixie tumbling to the floor. But that old boy hung onto my legs, digging his claws in.

"Ouch!" I gently removed his paws, making him relax his death grip on my legs, and looked up at Alec standing in front of me, looking at me curiously. I shook away the sleep and placed Dixie on the floor. "Apparently I was dozing." I took a chug of tepid coffee from my cup while he chuckled at me, and headed back to the kitchen, glancing at the clock. The cinnamon rolls had risen, and it was time to put them in the oven.

"What are you doing up so early?" he asked, following me into the kitchen.

I glanced over my shoulder at him. "Making cinnamon rolls. Doesn't that sound delicious?"

He nodded, his eyebrows shooting upward. "Yeah, it sounds very delicious. Where are they?" He sniffed the air.

I opened the oven door, pulled the pan out, and set it on the stovetop. "Right here. They need to bake for about thirty minutes." I carefully removed the parchment paper I had covered them with, trying to keep the tops from sticking to it. "Oh, these are going to be beauties." They were big and round, and gloriously filled with cinnamon and sugar, and just a hint of cardamom. I turned the oven on to preheat.

"Really? I've got to wait thirty minutes?" Alec said, heading to the coffeepot and pouring some coffee into a travel mug. "I've got to get down to the station."

"You're not going to want to leave just yet. If you do, you'll miss the cinnamon rolls."

He shook his head and went to the refrigerator, pouring a generous amount of creamer into his coffee. "I've got some reports to finish that I didn't take care of yesterday. I hate leaving things unfinished, but it got late last night, and I didn't want to stay longer than I already had. I really can't wait."

"Wait a minute, you're not seriously telling me that you're going to skip the cinnamon rolls?" I studied him. "Are you feeling okay?"

He looked indecisive. My husband loved his baked goods. "Couldn't you have gotten up a little bit earlier to make them?"

I made a face. "I was already up at 5:00. How early did you expect me to get up?"

He came closer and kissed me. Alec was tall and handsome with dark brown hair. "Four o'clock. The cinnamon rolls are made at 4:00 a.m. Just ask any professional baker."

I gasped in mock horror. "4:00 a.m. is not a time that any decent human being would be awake. If you really have to go, I can bring some by the station after Lucy and I go for a run. But they're not going to be hot and gooey. Not that it matters because they'll be just as tasty cold."

He eyed the pan of cinnamon rolls. "I love hot cinnamon rolls." He hesitated, thinking it over, then shook his head. "Nope. I've got to go. I don't want to leave things undone any longer than I have. But I sure would appreciate it if you would bring me some at the station."

I nodded and wiped my hands on a dish towel. "I'll bring a couple by for you, but I didn't make enough for the entire station, so you're going to have to keep quiet about them."

He nodded and kissed me again, then headed toward the door. "Mum's the word."

"Mum's the word," I muttered and put my coffee cup into the microwave to warm it up. I wasn't sure how long I had been dozing, but it couldn't have been more than ten or fifteen minutes. Twenty, tops. Or thirty. Dixie was weaving himself between my legs, waiting for the microwave to finish. "You already have enough food in your bowl, Mister. You don't need anymore."

Dixie meowed and looked forlornly at his nearly full bowl of crunchy cat food. He could look all he wanted; he wasn't getting any more food until this evening.

"Good morning," Lucy called out as she headed down the hallway to the kitchen.

"You're here early," I said.

She nodded. "Alec let me in. He said you're making cinnamon rolls."

I chuckled as I put the tray into the oven. "Get yourself a cup of coffee. We'll have cinnamon rolls shortly."

She went to the cupboard and got herself a cup. "The weather is beautiful outside. It's a little crisp out but not too cold yet. It's going to be perfect for a morning run. I'm so glad you made those cinnamon rolls. I'm starving." She went about making herself a cup of coffee.

I nodded and took a sip of my coffee. "Me too. They're awfully big though. I might only eat half of one before we go on our run. I'll save the rest for after we're done. I promised Alec I would bring him a couple of them after our run."

She eyed the oven door. "That doesn't look like enough for everybody at the station. You're going to give me a couple to bring home to Ed, aren't you?"

I nodded. "I told Alec to keep quiet about the cinnamon rolls. I'll have to make something to take down to the other officers at the police station in a couple of days." Making the officers something tasty had become a habit, one they looked forward to. It was good to keep the law happy and on your side.

She nodded. "I can hardly believe it's finally fall. I like summer just fine, but I love fall, and it felt like it took forever to get here."

I chuckled. "Fall never lasts long enough. You know how I feel about it. I want to stop by the home decor store later and pick up some more candles, and maybe a handful of things to decorate with. But we'll have to keep that our little secret because Alec thinks I've got more than enough things to decorate with."

Lucy chuckled and ran a hand through her short blond hair. "I don't know what's wrong with him. A woman can never have too many things to decorate with, especially when we're talking about fall decorating. I want to get some pumpkins from the farmer's co-op and some Indian corn, too."

"We'll have fun decorating."

A moment later, we heard footsteps coming down the stairs. Lucy and I looked at each other, eyebrows furrowed. "Is someone here with you?"

I shook my head. "Not that I'm aware of."

We hurried to the kitchen doorway where we could see the stairway. I was surprised to see my daughter, Jennifer, padding down the stairs in her pink fuzzy bathrobe and white bunny slippers on her feet.

"Jennifer, what are you doing here?" As far as I knew, she was in the next town over going to college. She should have been in class or getting ready for class right about now.

She stopped two steps from the bottom and looked at me sheepishly, then glanced at Lucy. "Oh. Sorry, I came in late last night, and I didn't want to wake you."

I stared at her, taking this in. It was Wednesday. Didn't she have classes? I was sure that she did. "Aren't you supposed to be at school? Will you make it in time if you leave now? But you're not even dressed." What was she thinking?

She took a deep breath and gave me a sleepy smile. "Mom, I changed my mind about school."

When she didn't continue, I said, "What do you mean you changed your mind about school? This is your last year. You're going to graduate in May."

She sighed and stepped down the last two stairs, moving toward us but not making eye contact. "Mom, I've had a change of plans. I want to do something different with my life."

"What are you talking about? Do you want to change your major?" She was going to school to be a biologist. It wasn't something that I'd ever had an interest in, so it was hard for me to understand why she wanted to do that, but I was behind her completely.

She shook her head. "Good morning, Lucy."

"Good morning, Jennifer," Lucy said, glancing worriedly at me.

Jennifer brushed past us into the kitchen, grabbed a coffee cup, and filled it. "Mom, I don't even know what I want to do with my life. I'm too young to make up my mind about what I want to do for the rest of my life, and I think I need to take some time off and figure things out." Her voice rose as she spoke, sounding frustrated.

I steeled myself against what I really wanted to say.

"Jennifer, you only have one more year. Then you will graduate, and you can figure out what you want to do. You can't just drop out of school. Is that what you did? I paid for college for this year. What are you doing?" Now *I* was frustrated. Her father and I had saved for our kids' education from the time they were born and the money had just stretched to her final year.

She sighed and went to the refrigerator and topped off her cup with creamer. "I know, Mom. I know. But it's been on my mind for a long time now and I don't know what I want to do. I don't want to be a biologist. I'm sure of that, but I don't know what it is that I want to do."

"But once you get your degree, you could do other things," Lucy pointed out. "You could be a teacher. You could do, I don't know, I'll kinds of things."

I nodded. "Honestly, Jennifer, you can't just drop out like this. Not only am I going to lose the money that I paid for college, but you're going to throw your education away, and you just can't do that."

She took a sip of her coffee, avoiding eye contact again. "I know, Mom. I know. I'm trying to sort things out, and I just don't know what I want to do with my life. I thought I wanted to be a biologist, but I was wrong. It isn't for me."

I took a deep breath. "Is it too late to get the tuition back? Is it past the drop date?"

She shrugged. "I'm not sure. I can call and find out."

She sounded entirely too casual about it, and I didn't like that one bit. I turned to Lucy. She looked just as surprised as I was.

CHAPTER 3

I inhaled the fresh fall air as we trotted down the road leading out of town. We normally ran on the running trail, at the beach, or in local neighborhoods, but I was dying to get closer to mother nature on our run this morning. If only the leaves had turned colors just a bit earlier, the morning would have been perfect. Not that it mattered because I loved being out here any time of year.

"I think we should make this our regular fall run until it gets too cold to run outside," Lucy said as we ran. The narrow paved road curved around the outside of town. It had been a frequently used road decades ago, but as the city had grown, it had been almost abandoned for use by automobiles and had been taken over by runners, bicycle riders, and the occasional horse rider. Only the people who lived nearby ever used it regularly anymore, so it was nice and quiet this morning. At one time, they wanted to connect this road with the running trail that ran through town, but the city had run out of funding to finish the paving that was required. The one thing they did manage to do was put in a few wrought iron benches along the way, where you could stop and rest if you needed to.

"I heard they were going to continue the repaving project in the spring and connect this road to the running path as they planned."

"I hope they do. This road could use a good facelift, and the potholes filled in." I hoped the plan went through.

"You know, if we get hungry, we could eat those cinnamon rolls you were going to take to Alec," Lucy said without looking at me.

I snorted. "No, because then we'd have to go back home and pack up some more cinnamon rolls to take to the station." We were halfway between the house and the police station. I didn't want to backtrack to get more cinnamon rolls.

She sighed dramatically. "All right then. We'll have to wait until we get back to your house to get more cinnamon rolls. They were absolutely delicious, not that I need to tell you that."

I chuckled. "I'm glad you told me that. It's always nice to hear that somebody appreciates my baking. I think it's the cardamom that adds that extra pizzazz."

"Well, I don't know what that is, but they are delicious."

We ran on in silence for a few minutes, each of us thinking our own thoughts. I didn't know what was up with Jennifer. We had packed her up and sent her off to school weeks ago. Of course, her college was only about forty-five minutes away from Sandy Harbor, and she made lots of frequent visits home, but she had her dorm room and all of her things put away just the way she liked them. Jennifer had always been my child with issues. Not that she was truly difficult. She was just more sensitive than her brother. It seemed that every decision she made was fraught with thoughts of how something might go wrong. I was surprised when she wanted to live in a dorm instead of coming home at the end of each school day, but I was glad, too. The independence had been good for her.

"What do you think is going on with Jennifer?" Lucy finally asked. I knew she had been thinking about it as much as I was.

I shook my head. "I don't know, but now is not a

great time to figure out that she chose the wrong major. I mean, she can just pick something else, right? She doesn't have to be a biologist. To be honest, I always thought that was a lofty goal, not that she isn't smart, but it was a lot of schooling, and I wondered whether she would enjoy that. She was never enthusiastic about high school."

She nodded as we ran on. Now and then, a leaf would drop from one of the trees and land near my feet. Each time it did, it made me just a little bit happier, knowing that fall—official fall—was closer.

"I hope she hasn't dropped out of her classes yet. I think she's going to figure out later that it's a mistake. She can change her major. Maybe she'll have to spend an extra year in school to catch up on whatever the new major is, but she doesn't have to throw away all of her schooling."

I nodded, huffing and puffing as we picked up our pace a bit. "Exactly. I know that if she does drop out, it's not like her class credits just disappear. They'll still be there, but sometimes the longer you stay away from school, the less likely you are to return, and I don't want her stuck in some dead-end job that she'll regret."

She nodded. "Maybe you and Alec can sit down and talk with her tonight. If she can just hang on for a bit longer, she might change her mind."

"I hope so."

We ran on in silence again. Clouds skated across the blue sky, and I wondered if we might get rain later in the day. The birds in the trees chirped loudly as we passed.

"I wonder what's going on up there?" I said when I caught sight of someone sitting on one of the benches ahead. We weren't close enough to be able to see if we knew who it was.

Lucy's head jerked up, and she squinted. "I don't know. I can't tell who it is. Looks like a man."

I nodded, and we continued running. I kept my eyes on him, squinting. It looked like he was reading a newspaper. *A newspaper?* That was an odd thing to be doing out here in the middle of nowhere. Lucy must have had the same thought at the same time that I did because we both came to a stop and waited, looking at him.

"Why doesn't he move?" she whispered.

I shook my head. "I don't know. Maybe he's engrossed in a lengthy article."

"Why would he be reading a newspaper out here? That's odd."

"I was thinking the same thing. I have no idea."

I looked back in the direction we had come, but the road was empty. I doubted many people came out here to go running. They should have, because it was beautiful, but it looked like we were alone at the moment.

We began walking toward the man. Something about him gave me the creeps.

"That must be a long article," Lucy said.

I nodded. "Maybe it's an in-depth article about cleaning your gutters."

She snorted, shaking her head. "The best tip I know for cleaning your gutters is to hire somebody to do it for you."

We kept walking, and I realized that it was indeed a man. But he wasn't moving that I could see. The hair stood up on my arms as we got closer. I didn't like this situation, and it probably would have been smarter to turn around and go back in the direction we had come from, but I was curious. One day that curiosity might get me killed.

We glanced at one another and kept walking. I pulled my phone from my pocket, and Lucy did the same. When we got closer, we stopped and gazed at the man. He was wearing a baseball cap pulled down over his ears and was bundled up in a heavy coat, one much heavier than was warranted in this weather. There were gloves on his hands, and he was holding the newspaper in front of his face so that we couldn't see it.

"Maybe he needs help," I whispered, knowing that

probably wasn't it. No, something else was going on here. "Turn the page," I breathed as we continued walking toward him. When we got closer, we stopped. "Good morning!" I called out. When the man still didn't move, Lucy and I looked at each other. "Good morning!" I said louder.

The man just stared at his newspaper.

"Hello!" Lucy called. "Are you okay? Do you need any help?"

The man didn't make a move.

This was more than just a little creepy. We should have left, but we were here, and I needed to figure out what was going on, so we moved a few steps closer. "Good morning!" When the man still didn't move, we moved in closer. "Are you alright?" We were standing a few feet in front of him now, and I realized by the color of his skin that something was very, very wrong here.

I dialed Alec. "Hello?"

"Alec, we went running on that road outside of town just past Langston Drive, and there's a man out here—I took a deep breath—and he doesn't look quite right."

As I spoke, my eyes were on the man, but he gave no indication of hearing me.

"What do you mean, not quite right?"

"I think maybe he has passed on."

"Dead," Lucy said.

"Was he hit by a car? What happened?"

"No, he wasn't hit by a car. He's sitting here reading his newspaper, and he appears to be dead. Unless he's in a coma, because he isn't answering us, and I suppose we can get closer to take a better look, but I'm going to be honest with you and tell you that I really don't want to do that."

"I'll be right there. Be careful of your surroundings."

"We'll be careful all right." I ended the call and gripped my phone tightly.

Lucy took two more steps closer to him. "Sir? Are you all right? Should we call an ambulance for you?" There was no response. A breeze suddenly came up, rattling his newspaper, and it slipped from his gloved hands. We screamed and ran back in the direction we had come from.

CHAPTER 4

*O*ne of the last things you expect to see is a dead guy on your morning run. Stranger things have happened, but I wasn't accustomed to finding dead bodies this early in the morning.

"Did you see anybody strange in the area?"

I stared at the dead guy, barely registering the question.

"Allie?"

I turned to look at Alec. He had his notebook and pen out and was waiting for my answer.

I shook my head. "We didn't see anybody out here. We parked at that empty lot on Trenton Street and started our run from there, but we didn't pass anybody."

"It was actually nice and peaceful out here this morning," Lucy agreed. "What happened to that guy?"

Alec made a quick note in his notebook and shoved it into his pocket. "Judging by the bloodstain on his shirt, he was either shot or stabbed, but I'm just taking a stab at that." He chuckled at his pun.

I rolled my eyes at him. "He looks familiar." The other officers hadn't arrived yet, but they would be here any moment, and then we would have to skedaddle.

"Why were you running out here?" Alec asked as he moved in closer to the body.

It was strange. The guy was sitting up with a newspaper in his hands, as if he were sitting on a park bench, just enjoying his morning. But I was betting that his morning hadn't gone to plan since he had ended up dead.

"Why is he sitting up like that? Why didn't he collapse when he was shot or stabbed? Why is he still holding onto his newspaper? What was he doing out here in the middle of nowhere?" These were questions that kept running through my mind, and I needed answers.

Alec shook his head. "That, my dear, is something that I'll have to figure out. You didn't answer my question."

I turned to look at him. "What question?"

"You usually run along the beach or on the running path. Why were you out here?"

"And we run through neighborhoods a lot," Lucy said.

I shrugged. "We thought it would be pretty to run out here with all the trees starting to change colors. We probably should have waited another couple of weeks though, because the leaves aren't as far along in their color change as I had hoped. Why?"

He shrugged. "I'm a detective. I've got to ask questions." He leaned closer to take a look at the dead guy. "Do either of you know who this is?"

I stepped closer. He looked familiar, but I couldn't quite put my finger on it. "I don't know, but I know I've seen him around. There's a coffee cup from the Cup and Bean next to him on the bench. There's a little dirt on it."

We heard sirens in the distance and glanced in that direction.

Lucy stepped in closer, making a face as she looked at the dead guy. "Oh, I know who this is. It's Jack Johnston. Ed worked with him a few years ago at the computer store in Bangor."

"Jack Johnston? I know him." I looked at the man again. He wore sunglasses and had grown a beard since I last saw him. "Any idea why he would be killed out here?"

She shook her head. "No. Ed mentioned him a month or two ago. Said he ran into him at the grocery store, and they talked for a few minutes. He said his father had passed away last year and he was trying to cope with that."

"I wonder if he came out here frequently. Maybe he enjoyed the fall leaves as much as we do." I wrapped my arms around myself. The morning had turned a bit chillier than I had anticipated, and I wished I had worn a light windbreaker.

"I doubt somebody comes out here just to read the newspaper," Alec said as he knelt to examine the area around the victim's feet. He took pictures of the ground as he worked. The sirens got louder, and I stepped closer to Alec to see what he was looking at.

"Do you see anything interesting?"

He shook his head. "Not yet. We'll have to wait to see what the medical examiner says about how he died and how long ago he thinks it was. That will give us a little more information. But I'm willing to bet he wasn't killed out here."

Lucy gasped. "You think he was killed somewhere else, and the killer brought his body out here?"

He looked up at her. "As I said, I don't think he came out here just to read his newspaper, and then somebody came along and killed him. It's an odd situation, don't you think?"

She nodded, crossing her arms in front of herself. "It is an odd situation. Why is he holding onto that newspaper?" Her eyes widened, and she gasped again. "What was he reading? Maybe it will give us a clue to the killer."

I sucked in air and went around the dead guy to look over his shoulder. "There's a sale on coffee at the grocery store."

Alec smirked, shaking his head.

Lucy groaned. "Oh, come on, he's got to be looking at something more interesting than that."

My eyes scanned the newspaper he held. It was from our small town, and to be perfectly honest, there weren't a lot of interesting things in it. There rarely was. "There's a short article on the upcoming Halloween bazaar. Other than that, there's not much. Peewee football is going to have their first game this Saturday."

"Maybe he was a fan of peewee football," Lucy said. "Maybe he knows somebody on one of the teams."

I had to say it wasn't a bad idea, but still, if he had been murdered someplace else and placed out here, then why would the killer open the newspaper to an article that might give more information about the victim? Unless, of course, it gave information about the killer, in which case it wasn't a bad idea at all. I checked the date on the newspaper. It was this morning's paper. "We need to get a hold of a copy of this newspaper."

She nodded. "There has to be something in it."

The first police car appeared as it came around the bend in the road. It shut off its sirens, pulled to the side, parked, and the officer got out. It was Yancey Tucker. "Morning, Alec," he said, then glanced at Lucy and me. He gave us a nod. "Morning, ladies."

"Good morning," I said. "I haven't seen you around in forever, Yancey. It's good to see you."

He smiled. "Thanks, Allie. You need to stop by the station more often and bring us cupcakes."

I sighed. "I know. I've been shirking my duties lately."

Yancey eyed Alec. "What have we got?"

Alec looked up at him. "Dead guy." He grinned. "I'm willing to bet he was killed someplace else and brought out here."

Yancey eyed the dead guy. "It's a weird setup. I wonder what the killer had in mind when they brought him out here like this."

"His name is Jack Johnston," Lucy supplied. "My husband knew him."

Yancey looked surprised. "I knew Jack. Not very well, but he was a nice guy."

Alec took a closer look around the bench where

Jack was sitting and took more photos. Then he seemed to remember the two of us and turned to look at us. "Allie, Lucy, I think you better finish your run in town. We're going to be out here working the scene for a while."

I knew what that meant. He wanted us to skedaddle so we weren't in the way. That was fine. We had a murder to look into now. I nodded. "Sure, I guess we had better get going if we want to finish our run." I glanced at Lucy and she nodded. We turned and headed back in the direction we had come from as more police officers arrived on the scene.

"I'm trying to remember everything Ed told me about Jack," Lucy said as we walked. "His father died not long ago, but his mother was still alive."

I nodded. "I think we should talk with his mother then. What's her name? Do you know her?"

She nodded. "Sure, her name is Margaret Johnston. She used to enter a lot of those baking contests that you used to enter a few years back."

"Oh," I said, nodding. "I know her. She's a nice lady. I hate that she recently lost her husband, and now she's going to find out that her son was murdered. Did Ed say how his father died?"

She shook her head. "No, I was under the impression it was natural causes, but I'll ask him again."

We walked down the road for a bit, and after a few

minutes, we broke into a trot. I wasn't in the mood to run anymore, but we were still more than a mile from my car, and we had some investigating to do.

"I guess you don't have to take the cinnamon rolls to Alec at the station. He won't be there for a while. We had better go home and make sure they don't go to waste."

I eyed Lucy. "The cinnamon rolls aren't going to go to waste. But I hear you, I could do with another cinnamon roll."

My cinnamon rolls had turned out quite good this morning, and I was keen on getting back home to have another one. We'd have to give Jack's mother a few more days before going to see her, so maybe I would whip up another batch and take some to her. I glanced over my shoulder at Alec and the officers going over the crime scene. It was an odd situation. Jack, sitting there reading that newspaper, dead as he was.

CHAPTER 5

*B*efore heading home, we decided to stop by the Cup and Bean Coffee Shop for a pumpkin spice latte to warm ourselves up. We still had the cinnamon rolls sitting at home, calling our names, and as tempting as they were, I just wanted to get a coffee first. We hadn't gotten the run that we had planned, but when your run is cut short by finding a dead guy, you just have to go with the flow.

"It sure does smell good in here," Lucy said when we walked through the doors of the coffee shop.

I nodded. "Doesn't it though? I swear I missed my calling. I should have been a barista."

"We should have opened a coffee shop together," Lucy said, looking up at the menu board as we got into the short line at the front counter. "You could

34

have made all the baked goods, and I could have made the coffee. We would have made a great team."

"It's not a bad idea," I said. "Maybe we should think about doing that."

She frowned. "No, that would be too much work. I'm in my retirement years, you know."

I laughed at her. "You're not old enough to be in your retirement years yet."

She grinned. "We'll just call it early retirement then. I was thinking about getting another part-time job, but that would take up too much of my time."

I chuckled. "I was thinking the same thing. I miss baking more regularly. I'm going to have to come up with something. I only watch the baby occasionally, and I don't get to spend nearly as much time as I would like with her, so I've got some free time."

She turned and looked at me as we moved forward in line. "Why don't you watch her full-time? Sarah would let you do that, wouldn't she?"

I shrugged. "I'm sure she would, but the baby is doing really well with the woman who is watching her now. I don't want to butt my nose in there and cause issues."

We had the baby at least one weekend a month, and then there were holidays and other days that the kids stopped by with her. It wasn't like I never got to see her. But there were days that I wished I had more to do with my time. It had been a while since I had a real job, and it would have been nice to do something. I still occasionally got orders from people who wanted me to bake something for a special occasion, and that was a lot of fun. I was thinking maybe I should advertise my services and pick up a few more jobs.

We placed our orders for pumpkin spice lattes, and I looked over at the corner table where our friend Mr. Winters sat. He raised his cup of black coffee in greeting—I knew it was black because it was almost all he ever drank. I nodded and smiled, and we headed over and sat at his table. "Good morning, Mr. Winters," I said. I reached under the table and patted his little gray poodle on the head. Sadie licked my fingers and wagged her stump of a tail.

"Good morning, ladies." He leaned forward over the table.

I spotted his newspaper on the table. "Good morning, Mr. Winters. Do you mind if I take a look at your newspaper?"

"Help yourself."

I snatched the newspaper and opened it up, turning to the page that had the grocery store ad. If there was anything in here that would lead to the killer, I was going to find it.

"I heard sirens about thirty minutes ago. What's up?"

Lucy and I glanced at each other. "There are sirens all over this town throughout the day," I said and took a sip of my coffee.

He nodded. "But they were headed toward the outskirts of town. They don't frequently go out in that direction. What's going on? I can see it written all over your faces. Something happened."

"You better let him in on it," Lucy said. "He won't give you a moment's rest if you don't."

I leaned forward. "There's been a murder."

His face lit up. "Ha! I knew it. Who is it? We've got work to do."

I shook my head. "I can't tell you that. It's still fresh, and the relatives have not been notified." I didn't envy Alec that job. He was going to have to talk to Jack Johnston's family and let them know that he had been murdered. I shuddered.

He sighed and took a sip of his black coffee. "I can't believe that you're playing hard to get. After all the help that I've given you these past several years?"

He was right. Mr. Winters could sometimes come up with information that was important in solving a murder case. "Okay, but do you swear you're going to keep it to yourself?"

He nodded. "Cross my heart."

That was one thing I could rely on Mr. Winters for. He kept names to himself. He had sources he got information from, and he still had never told me their names. "Jack Johnston."

His eyes widened. "Really?" he said thoughtfully.

I nodded. "Yes, he was out on that empty road past Langston Drive."

He took a sip of his coffee, taking this in. "What happened?"

I shook my head. "We don't know. He's dead though." I wanted to keep the details of the murder to myself for now. I didn't know what Alec wanted to release to the public.

"Did you know him?" Lucy asked, leaning forward.

He nodded. "Sure. I knew him, but I guess not well. I ran into him at the Seashore Diner several times a week."

"Several times a week?" I asked.

He nodded. "You don't think I do my own cooking, do you? I do very little of it and I like to stop by the Seashore Diner a few days a week for lunch. They have good burgers, and their meatloaf is out of this world."

I nodded. "Apparently Jack didn't do his own cooking either then."

"No, and you can't judge a man for that. Some of

us just don't enjoy cooking, but we do enjoy eating, so the solution is to have somebody else do it for us." He chuckled.

"What about his wife? Didn't she do any cooking?" Lucy asked.

He shrugged. "I don't know. You'd have to ask her."

"Any ideas who might have killed him?" I asked.

He sat thinking for a few moments before answering. "I don't know. I do know he has an uncle who doesn't like him though. Hal Johnston. Do you know him?"

I tried to think of who he might be talking about, but I shook my head. "I don't think so. Who is he? Where does he work?"

"Wait a minute, the mobile car wash service guy?" Lucy asked.

He nodded. "That's him. He'll come out to your house and give your car a thorough cleaning inside and out for twenty-five dollars. It's a bargain."

"What? He'll clean your car inside and out for twenty-five dollars?" I asked. "How come I didn't know about this?" I had been taking my car to the do-it-yourself one in town. It only cost two dollars, but as the name implied, you have to do it yourself. Vacuuming the inside was extra money and extra work.

He shrugged. "I don't know. But you're missing out because he does an excellent job."

"Wait a minute, how old is this guy? I think Jack must be in his early to mid-fifties. If Hal is his uncle, how old is he?"

He shook his head. "I don't know. Maybe seventy or seventy-five? But he's in good shape. He doesn't move like he's that old. I think sometimes when you quit working too early, you age a lot faster," he said. "That's why I worked until I was seventy." He flexed his biceps for us.

I nodded. He had a point about that. "Okay, so what does this Hal Johnston say about his nephew?"

"Only that he was lazy and shiftless. I don't know what the trouble between them was because I just wanted my car washed. But Hal likes to talk. He's one of those people who talk all the time."

"At least that gives me someplace to start. Maybe I'll give Hal Johnston a call to come out and wash my car. Since he's a talker, it might not be too hard to get him to talk about his nephew. But remember, he doesn't know that he's dead yet," I warned.

He nodded. "Duly noted. I won't whisper a word about his death until it becomes well known. And that won't take long. You know how it is around here."

"I know. Everybody's going to be talking about this. Did he say anything else about his nephew?"

He shrugged. "He said that when Jack's father—Hal's brother—Andrew died, he was shocked because he had expected a large inheritance from him. It seems that Andrew Johnston made a lot of money in the stock market and was quite well off. He promised Hal that he would leave him money in the will. Andrew was the oldest in the family, and Hal was the youngest with quite an age span, as I understand it. So he was expecting a lot of money, but when the will was read, it turned out that he didn't inherit nearly as much money as he thought he would. He blames Jack for that, but I'm not exactly sure why."

Lucy turned to me. "Well, there you go. There's a motive for murder right there. Money. People always turn greedy when the will is read."

She wasn't wrong about the greedy part. "Maybe. It's certainly something we need to check into."

Mr. Winters looked at his watch. "Well, ladies, I hate to run, but I have an orthodontist appointment."

Lucy and I looked at him. "An orthodontist appointment?" I asked, puzzled.

He nodded and smiled, showing silver braces on his teeth. His white mustache had been hiding them. "I've been meaning to do this for decades, and I finally got around to it. My doctor gave me a clean bill of health last month, and I figure I might live forever, so why not do it with nice teeth?"

I chuckled. "There's no reason why you shouldn't."

"I'm jealous," Lucy said. "I always wanted braces, but my mother said my teeth were straight enough. These days, though, people expect perfect teeth. Mine are anything but perfect."

"Your teeth are nice," I said.

He nodded and got to his feet. "Well, I better get going. I've got to drop Sadie off at the house before I get to my appointment. Let me know how things shake out with Hal Johnston."

"I certainly will. Oh, can I have the newspaper?"

"Oh, sure. I'm done with it." He left with Sadie trailing behind him.

If Hal Johnston was unhappy about having his share of his brother's will reduced, and he blamed it on his nephew Jack, it might be enough to commit murder.

CHAPTER 6

*I*t had been several days since Lucy and I had found Jack Johnston's body down at the edge of town. I'd poured over the newspaper Mr. Winters had given me but couldn't find anything that pointed to the killer.

Alec was working on the case, and I was working on my cinnamon roll recipe. Not that it needed any improvement because in my opinion, such as it is, I thought they were pretty perfect. But saying that I was working on the recipe gave me an excuse to make more of them. I had taken a large batch of them to the police station, and the feedback had been quite positive. There's nothing like hearing that somebody enjoys your cinnamon rolls when you put so much effort into them.

"The cinnamon rolls sure smell good," Lucy said, inhaling. "I swear I could eat half a dozen of them every day for the rest of my life."

I chuckled. "In that case, you'll have to do an awful lot of running for the rest of your life."

She sighed. "I've learned to enjoy running, or at least tolerate it, but not enough to run off the calories from half a dozen cinnamon rolls every day. I guess I'm going to have to just stick with eating them as a treat now and then."

I nodded as I parked in front of Margaret Johnston's house. Margaret was Jack's mother, and I wanted to check on her to see how she was holding up as well as see what she had to say about the murder. "A treat now and then is easier to run off than a habit."

We got out of the car and walked up to the door. I knocked, and we waited.

Margaret opened the door and looked surprised to see us standing there. She blinked twice. "Yes?"

I smiled. "Hello, Margaret," I said, pausing in the hopes she would recognize us.

Her eyes widened. "Oh, hello, Allie. Hello, Lucy."

I nodded. "Margaret, we wanted to stop by to see how you were doing, and to tell you how sorry we were about what happened to your son."

"Yes, we're so sorry, Margaret. How are you doing?"

Her scowl deepened. "Well, how do you think I'm doing? Somebody murdered my son." Her voice cracked on the word 'murdered.'

"I'm so sorry," I said again. "Is there anything we can do for you? I brought you some cinnamon rolls, and if there's anything we can do, we certainly would like to help out."

She softened. "That's nice of you. Would you like to come in?"

I nodded, and we followed her into the house.

Margaret's house looked like it hadn't been updated since the 1950s. She had those cute lamps with frilly lampshades and Danish modern furniture.

We sat down on the sofa that she indicated, and she sat across from us. "I spoke to your husband the other day," she said slowly. "You are married to the detective, aren't you?"

I nodded, and Lucy set the cinnamon rolls on the white cherry wood coffee table. "Yes, Alec is my husband. I know he's doing everything he can to find your son's killer."

She sighed. "He said he doesn't have any idea yet who killed him. I don't understand it. My son was a good boy. He was always so helpful as a child, and he was a good student. He always worked hard at everything he took on. I just don't know who could have killed him. Or why? It makes no sense."

Lucy nodded. "My husband worked with your son years ago. He liked him very much."

She sighed. "He was always a good worker. Always. It isn't right." She suddenly teared up and reached for a tissue from the box on the coffee table, dabbing at her eyes. "I spoke to his wife, Merlene, and she's just devastated. As is their daughter, Bella. I don't know how we will survive this."

I nodded. "He didn't mention to anyone that he may have been having trouble with someone?"

She shook her head. "No. Not at all. I think it had to be a random killer who came to town, and my poor son happened to cross paths with him." She shook her head. "Just something random."

I nodded, but I knew that wasn't the case. The killer had taken the time to take his body out to that bench on the edge of town and set him up as if he were reading his newspaper. Why do that? It wasn't the work of a stranger. It was the work of someone who was trying to make some sort of point. But I didn't know what that point was yet.

"So he wasn't having any trouble with anyone?" Lucy asked.

She shook her head. "Oh, I suppose he and his wife did have some issues. Don't all married couples?

Before my husband Andrew died, we went round and round occasionally. But it was very occasional, so I don't imagine you could say it was serious enough that he wanted to murder me." She smiled, but it was an odd smile that made me wonder if she was telling the truth.

"All married couples have trouble from time to time," Lucy agreed. "Ed and I, we don't agree on much of anything, but we still manage to live together just fine. I know he has a good heart, and he loves me, and I feel the same way toward him."

She nodded eagerly. "Yes. Exactly like that. When you know that your spouse loves you, you can put up with an awful lot." She chuckled. "My Andrew was difficult at times. But he was a good man. He worked hard at his job, and he did his best to provide for our family. Jack took after him in so many ways and I couldn't have been more proud of him."

"Of course," I agreed. "Couples argue all the time." But why was I getting the feeling that there might have been more than that? It was the look on her face when she brought up that Jack and his wife had problems occasionally. Something was going on there. "So, he told you that he and his wife were having difficulties?"

She nodded. "Yes, he always confided in me. I was the one person that he knew he could talk to about

47

anything that was on his mind, and that I wouldn't tell anyone else. He did that frequently, you know. Came to me for advice on life issues."

She reached up and touched her white, closely cropped hair. "A child that can trust their mother is a more stable individual," I said carefully. I had the feeling Margaret may have been more involved in her son's life than she should have been, but I didn't want her to think there was something wrong with that. I wanted to see what else she had to say about it. "So if he was having some issues, he would have come to you."

She nodded too eagerly. "Yes, of course. I was his best friend. That's how I knew they were having some issues, and he was honestly perplexed by it. He was going to work every day, working as hard as he could, and his wife didn't seem to appreciate it. I like Merlene, but sometimes she's just wrong about the way she treated him. She didn't respect him enough. She didn't look to him to make the important decisions in their marriage, as I did with my Andrew. When you don't do that, it causes problems in the marriage. Take my word on it. If you ladies don't look to your husbands to make important decisions for you, you're going to have trouble."

I felt Lucy stiffen. I hoped she wouldn't say anything to put Margaret off, but Lucy just smiled and nodded. "That's exactly right. A man needs to feel like he's the one in charge." She shot me a look.

Margaret smiled again. "That's right, ladies. Always allow your husband to feel that he's the one in charge. Even if we are ultimately going to be running the household and raising the children, he has to feel like he is in charge. And poor Jack just wasn't in charge of that household." She frowned.

"Oh? More than just disagreements with his wife?" I asked. I was thankful that Margaret was talkative, and now I felt like we were getting somewhere. If Jack believed as his mother did—that he was supposed to wear the pants in the family—and his wife didn't feel the same way, there were going to be problems.

She nodded. "That daughter of his is just a mess. So rebellious," she said, shaking her head. "I never understood it. I never had a day of trouble with my kids, but poor Jack put up with so much that he shouldn't have had to. If his wife had raised their daughter properly, she wouldn't have rebelled against her father."

"How old is Bella? Do they only have one child?" I asked.

"Yes, just the one. That was another point of contention for them. Jack wanted at least three, but Merlene only wanted one. Bella is nineteen."

"Oh, so she's an adult now?"

She nodded. "Yes, she's an adult. Not that she behaves that way. Honestly, I don't know how she's gotten on in life this far. Now, I hope you'll excuse me, but I've got to make arrangements at the church for the meal after the funeral. I can't even rely on his wife to do that." She shook her head. "That woman. I don't know what she's thinking."

"Oh, we understand," I said, nudging Lucy. We stood up, and she saw us to the door. I turned to her as we stepped outside. "Now, Margaret, don't hesitate to give us a call if you need anything."

"Yes, we'll be here if you need anything," Lucy assured her.

She smiled. "I certainly appreciate that. You ladies are so sweet to stop by. And I will enjoy those cinnamon rolls, Allie. Thank you."

"You're welcome." We headed back to my car.

When we got inside, Lucy and I looked at one another. "That was strange," she said.

I nodded. "Margaret is far too involved in her son's life. She said she was his best friend. It makes me wonder how much trouble that caused in his marriage." I started the car and pulled away.

"Exactly."

CHAPTER 7

*A*lec leaned over and kissed me. "How is my beautiful wife doing?"

I grinned as I kneaded the cinnamon roll dough. "I'm doing fantastic. How is my smart, handsome, wonderfully sweet husband doing?"

"Can you cut back on the lovey-dovey talk?" Thad said from where he sat at the kitchen table. He had a cup of coffee in front of himself and a half-eaten cinnamon roll.

I shook my head. "No."

His wife, Sarah, smiled. "I think it's sweet. I hope we're still that way after we've been married for a while."

I looked at her. "We haven't been married that long."

She gently jiggled the baby on her knee. "I know, but I still hope that we have that kind of sweetness in twenty years."

"Well, if Mr. Sourpuss over there doesn't straighten up, you won't." I shot Thad a look.

He rolled his eyes dramatically and sighed. "Fine, I'll work on my sweetness."

I chuckled as I placed the dough into a bowl to rise. I had received several orders for cinnamon rolls from the officers after I had dropped off a box of them at the station. Sometimes it pays to hand out samples, although I hadn't intended them to be samples. But it was nice that people enjoyed them so much they wanted to buy them.

"I heard you were working on a case, Alec," Sarah said. Little Lilly sat in her lap, trying to reach her toes. Her tongue darted out between her lips with her effort, making me chuckle.

He nodded. "I am. It seems your mother-in-law and her nosy friend just happened to run into a dead body the other day."

"Imagine that," Thad said.

I sighed. "Lucy isn't nosy."

"I stand corrected. Your mother-in-law is the nosy one."

I swatted at him with a dish towel. "Lucy and I

went out there for our morning exercise. Don't act like we were looking for trouble."

He grinned. "No, but it's amazing how often trouble finds you."

Thad laughed. "Way to go, Mom."

"Have you found out anything new about the case?" I asked, ignoring their comments.

He shrugged. "The medical examiner says he was shot, and we sent the newspaper in for testing for fingerprints. His sunglasses were wiped clean."

"Really?" I said thoughtfully. "They knew enough to wipe down his sunglasses, but I wonder if they knew enough to do something about the newspaper? Maybe they thought their fingerprints wouldn't transfer to the newspaper."

"They might have been wearing gloves," Sarah pointed out.

Alec nodded. "They might have been, but I'm betting they weren't because they took the time to wipe down the sunglasses. We'll see."

"What about his wallet? Was he robbed?" Thad asked and took a sip of his coffee.

He shook his head. "It looks like everything was in his wallet. His driver's license, credit cards, and a little bit of cash were all still there."

I sighed. We needed to know more about his final hours before he died. "Did the medical examiner say when he died?" I was very interested in that information. Lucy and I had been out at the edge of the woods around 10:30 a.m., later than usual, since we had stopped to eat a cinnamon roll before leaving the house. When had Jack Johnston died? How long had he been out there? Could it have been days since it wasn't a busy road anymore? Or just a few hours?

"The medical examiner thinks it was only about two to three hours before you found him."

I turned to him. "Oh. If Lucy and I had gone for our run earlier, we might have been able to prevent his murder." My heart sank.

"Or you might have been faced with the killer, and become victims," Sarah pointed out.

Alec nodded. "That's true. It's a good thing you made cinnamon rolls that morning."

I went to the coffee pot to pour myself a cup. Sarah was right, but I still felt badly that he had died not long before we arrived. "Okay then, he was killed some time that morning and dumped out there in the woods. It's just so odd that he was placed the way he was. Don't you think so?" I got some creamer out of the refrigerator and poured it into my cup. Pumpkin spice. I could never get enough pumpkin spice.

"Oh, it's weird, all right," Alec said. He took a sip of his coffee and kissed Lilly on top of her head, then sat down. "It makes you wonder why somebody went to the effort to do that."

Sarah shook her head. "It's creepy." We'd filled Thad and Sarah in on some of the details, and I had to admit that it was indeed creepy.

"How much longer for the cinnamon rolls, Mom?" Thad was finishing up the last one from my last batch.

I shrugged. "It's going to be awhile. The dough has to rise, and then they've got to bake. And you just ate one. But it's early yet, so you three can just hang out here with us." We had already finished dinner, and I had decided to make some more cinnamon rolls. They had eaten before they came over, so we had time to hang out and relax. I loved evenings like this. A breeze was blowing outside and more leaves fell from the trees. It had gotten chillier than the weatherman had predicted, so it was a wonderful, cozy evening. Perfect for hanging out with the family in a warm kitchen.

"Okay, but if we've got to sit and wait that long, I'm going to expect to bring some home." Thad looked at me, one eyebrow raised.

I rolled my eyes, took the baby from Sarah, and sat next to Alec. "You act like it's a chore to be here with your mother."

He sighed. "It's only a chore if I don't get cinnamon rolls."

Sarah gave him a playful shove. "You should treat your mother better than that."

He chuckled. "Sorry, it is a delight to be here this evening, Mother. I am so glad we decided to drop by."

Sarah looked at me. "That was the first thing he said when he got home from work. He wanted to come and see you. Don't listen to his teasing."

I beamed. My boy wanted to spend time with me. "I raised my boy right."

"You sure did, and I am happy about that," she said and took a sip of her coffee.

We all turned as Jennifer made an appearance in the kitchen doorway. The murder had taken my mind off of her, but only for a few moments at a time. I didn't know what she planned on doing, but I didn't want her to throw her education away.

"Oh. What's going on in here?"

"We are waiting for cinnamon rolls," Thad said. "What are you doing?"

She brightened. "There are more cinnamon rolls?"

"They're rising, so it's going to be a bit before they're ready," I said. "But your niece is here to see you."

She grinned. "Come here, you beautiful girl," she said, holding her arms out to her and taking her from me. "Look how pretty you are. You look just like your aunt."

Thad laughed. "Stop it. She looks like her father."

Jennifer eyed him. "You've lost your mind." She bounced Lilly on her hip and went to look in the refrigerator. She had been making herself scarce since showing up at the house the other day and hadn't come down for dinner.

"There's some spaghetti in the refrigerator if you want to reheat it in the microwave," I told her.

She nodded. "I'm not hungry. I'm sure I will be for cinnamon rolls when they're ready though." She grinned at me.

"So, Jennifer, what are you doing with yourself these days?" Sarah asked. I had told Sarah and Thad about Jennifer wanting to drop out of school, and Sarah had a way with Jennifer. The two had become thick as thieves when Sarah entered our lives, and I was glad of it. If anybody could talk Jennifer into returning to school, it would be her.

Jennifer closed the refrigerator and came over and sat next to Sarah. "I'm trying to find myself. That's what they used to say back in the 60s. I've decided to take a trip back to the 60s and try to find myself." She chuckled, but it sounded flat.

Sarah nodded. "I'm all for finding yourself, and I

don't mean to nag, but what about school? Can't you find yourself in school?"

Jennifer's eyes went to the baby as she cooed at her. "I don't know. Honestly, I don't even know what's going on with myself these days." She made herself smile. "I guess I better make up my mind quickly, or I'm going to be in big trouble at the college."

"I don't want you losing that money," I said. I sounded like a broken record, but I couldn't help myself. It was important.

She nodded. "I have an appointment with my guidance counselor tomorrow."

I breathed a sigh of relief. Maybe her guidance counselor would give her ideas about what to do. If she wanted to change her major, that was fine. Even if it meant an extra year in college, at least she wouldn't lose all her credits. I wanted her to graduate college with the education that would help her to get the job she wanted.

"I think that's an excellent idea," I said. "Your counselor may have some great ideas for you."

"Do you have any idea what you want to do with your life?" Thad asked. "Anything? Being a teacher isn't so bad, you know. You could use most of your credits for a teaching degree."

She nodded. "I know. And I've thought about doing that, but I'm not sure it's what I want."

I got up to make the icing for the cinnamon rolls.

"You can do anything you want to do," Alec said. "Honestly, if you don't want to be a biologist, there's no sense in completing that degree. But as everyone else has said, don't drop out and waste the money that was paid on tuition."

She nodded without looking at him. "I'm not going to waste it. I swear. I just have to figure out what it is I want to do."

Making up her mind about anything was never easy for Jennifer, so this probably shouldn't have surprised me. But I would have rather this had come up in her freshman or sophomore year and not her senior year of college. It would be fine though. She would figure out what it was she wanted to do. At least, I hoped she would.

CHAPTER 8

The following day, I decided to drop by and speak to Jack Johnston's wife. She had to know what was going on in her husband's life before he died, didn't she? No one else would know as much as she would when it came to what her husband had been up to, so I boxed up half a dozen large cinnamon rolls to take to her.

Lucy and I decided to skip our morning run in favor of visiting the grieving widow. We had been logging a lot of miles on our runs, and we needed the break anyway, so this was a great excuse to take that break.

"I haven't seen Merlene in forever. I wonder what she's been up to?" Lucy asked idly as I pulled up to her house.

"You know, now that you mention it, I haven't seen her around either. I wonder what's going on with her." I glanced at the two-story red brick house. The yard was neatly trimmed and there was a large pumpkin near the entryway.

We headed up to the door, and I knocked. A woman answered the door before I could knock twice, and I hesitated. "Merlene?"

She nodded. "Yes?" She glanced at the box in Lucy's hand.

Merlene had changed since I last saw her. She had lost at least fifty pounds and her hair was now blond. Even in her grieving state, she was dressed nicely in what looked to be designer jeans and a silk blouse. I gave her a sympathetic smile. "We heard about Jack, and we wanted to stop by and tell you how sorry we are."

"We're very sorry for your loss. And Allie made some cinnamon rolls," Lucy said, holding the box out to her.

She smiled as tears came to her eyes. "Oh, aren't you the sweetest? You two are so wonderful to think about me this way. I still can't get over the fact that he was murdered. Would you like to come in?"

I nodded, and we followed her into the house.

"I'll take the cinnamon rolls from you," she said,

turning back to Lucy and taking the box. "Why don't we have a cup of coffee and a cinnamon roll?"

"That sounds great," I said, following her into the kitchen.

She set the table and got the pot of brewed coffee from the coffee maker, then set it on the table, along with some cream and sugar. "I tell you girls, this is not how I envisioned my life. I'm too young to be a widow. I can't imagine anyone killing Jack. It's not like he was one of those people who was always in some sort of trouble." She shook her head, fetched three coffee mugs and plates from the cupboard, and set them next to the coffee pot.

"I was shocked when I heard about it," Lucy said, pouring coffee into the cups. "He worked with my husband a few years ago, you know."

She nodded. "Yes, he mentioned your husband a time or two. But that was a long time ago, wasn't it? I don't know where the time goes. I don't know what I'm going to do without my husband," she said, frowning as she spooned sugar into her cup. "I lived for that man, you know? When he asked me to marry him, I was in heaven. We had been dating for nearly a year, and I knew from the first date that he was the man for me. And now somebody took him away from me." Her bottom lip trembled as she poured cream into her coffee.

"I'm so sorry," I said, adding sugar and cream to my coffee and giving her a moment to get herself together. "I can't imagine who would do something like that. Do you have any idea what might have happened to him?"

She looked up at me with tears in her eyes. "No. I talked to your husband the other day, and he about broke my heart when he told me what happened. I still can't get over it. I would never have expected him to end up murdered."

I nodded. "I feel so bad for Alec that he has to do that. Notifying next of kin about their family member's death, I mean."

She took a sip of her coffee. "It must be an awful job. I wouldn't have the heart to do it."

"It has to be a difficult thing to do," Lucy agreed. She glanced at me, wanting to dig into the meatier questions, but you had to be careful what and how you asked.

She helped herself to a cinnamon roll, and Lucy and I split one. We had brought her six, and they were oversized, so she would still have plenty of cinnamon rolls left.

She took a bite and nodded. "Oh, Allie, this cinnamon roll is delightful. My gosh, I don't think I've ever had one this tasty."

I smiled. "Thank you. I worked on that recipe for a

while. I think it's the cardamom in the filling and all the extra butter I used in the dough. It makes them so moist and rich. I'm glad you like it."

She nodded. "It's perfection. I swear, you could go into business selling them. Cinnabon down at the mall has nothing on you."

I chuckled. "Thank you. It's nice to hear that someone enjoys what I make." I hesitated a moment. "So, you don't have any idea who might have wanted to kill Jack?"

She sighed, not looking at me. "I hate to say it, and maybe I shouldn't." She hesitated. "But the only person that I could imagine who might have wanted to kill Jack is his uncle." She looked at me now. "I'm a terrible person for saying it. They were family, after all. But his uncle could be cantankerous, to say the least."

"But why would he want to kill him?" Lucy asked.

She took a sip of her coffee. "Because when Jack's father died, he was supposed to leave his brother, Hal, a large amount of money. At least, that's what Uncle Hal says. But Jack's father didn't leave him nearly as much as he thought it would be. And he was so angry that most of the money went to Jack."

"I can see how that would upset someone," I said. "But it wasn't Jack's decision, so why would he be angry at him?"

She shrugged. "I know it doesn't make sense, but some people are funny about money. It's all they care about, and they're just plain greedy if you ask me. And that's his uncle. He thought he was entitled to more money, but Jack's father had a good head on his shoulders. He knew exactly who he wanted to leave the money to, and he did."

"Who else got money in the will?" I asked.

"Was it a lot of money?" Lucy asked. I shot her a look. That was another question I wondered about, but I didn't want to seem too pushy.

She nodded. "Jack's father had invested in the stock market and made quite a bit of money over the years. Apparently, Uncle Hal got it in his head that his brother was going to give him a quarter of a million dollars. He claims he was told exactly how much it was going to be. A quarter of a million, and that it was a done deal. He said his brother put it in the will and everything."

"How much did he get?" Lucy asked.

"Ten thousand."

Now that was a big difference. "I can see where he would be angry about that," I said thoughtfully. "But why kill Jack over it? That wouldn't get him the money."

She sighed. "You would think he would under-stand that wouldn't you? But I guess he may have been led astray by Jack." She looked from me to Lucy and back. "Jack used to tease him by telling him he was going to put him in his own will to make up for the money he didn't get from his father's death. I told him he shouldn't tell him things like that, but he thought it was funny. I don't think Hal realized he was teasing him."

"That's an awful thing to do," Lucy said, cutting into her cinnamon roll with her fork. "And he thinks that he's still in Jack's will?"

She shook her head. "Uncle Hal wasn't going to get any money from Jack. I mean, when you think about it, if things had played out naturally, Uncle Hal would have died before Jack. Uncle Hal was the youngest in his family, only twenty years older than Jack, but still. Chances were good that he was going to die first. So it didn't make sense for Jack to put him in his will. Uncle Hal doesn't know yet that he wasn't going to get any money, and I'm afraid to tell him."

I shook my head. "No, it doesn't make sense for him to think he would inherit money from Jack. Unless Jack had had some sort of illness that would have taken his life earlier, chances were very good that Uncle Hal would have died first. But would Uncle Hal really think he could get away with Jack's murder and inherit some money? If he was as angry as you say about not inheriting the money from his brother, maybe. Some people are so obsessed with money that they don't think straight."

She nodded. "That's exactly how Uncle Hal is."

"I wonder if Alec has talked to Uncle Hal?" Lucy asked, turning to me.

I shrugged. "If he has, he hasn't mentioned it to me, but I know that he'll talk to everyone who might have wanted to kill Jack."

I didn't want to say anything specific in front of Merlene. The investigation was Alec's business, and I wasn't going to stick my nose into it. Well, maybe I would stick my nose into it, but I couldn't let a murder victim's wife know what I knew. All of this did make me wonder about Uncle Hal. Had he killed his nephew? Did he think he would make a lot of money if he was dead?

CHAPTER 9

I needed to talk to Hal Johnston. I felt certain he would have information that would help us make progress in the investigation to find his nephew's killer. It had been a while since my car had been thoroughly cleaned inside and out, so I called and made an appointment for him to come by the house and take care of it. This also gave me an excuse to hang out, watch him work, and hopefully gather the information that I needed.

Hal showed up at 11:00, just as he promised, with his truck and a small trailer that housed a spray washer. He got straight to work setting up his equipment.

"I'm so glad you could come out on such short notice," I said. "I've been telling my husband for weeks now that my car is just filthy, and I need it cleaned. But of course, I've been too busy to take it down to the car wash myself." I chuckled. "Not to mention, that's not one of my favorite jobs anyway."

He smiled and nodded. "No, ma'am, it's not many people's favorite thing to do. That's why I'm here. I don't mind doing the dirty work. We can even set up a regular schedule if you'd like."

I crossed my arms in front of myself and smiled. "Well, I can't tell you how happy that makes me. I don't know why I haven't called you sooner. What's more convenient than having the car wash come right to my door?" I chuckled.

He nodded again as he got his spray washer ready.

"I give a special deal to my best customers. After twelve washes, the thirteenth is free. You just give me a call whenever you need me. Lots of folks are set up for regular visits. Helps to make their lives easier."

Hal Johnston looked to be in his 70s, but he moved with ease. His skin was sun-weathered from being outside for his job, and when he smiled, he revealed bright white teeth. A blue baseball cap was pulled down over his white hair.

"Well, you know I'm going to take advantage of that offer then. I'll ask my husband when he wants his car done, and we'll get to that thirteenth free car wash quickly."

"You do that," he said as he turned to my car. "If you're not satisfied with the job, then I'll do it until it's done right."

I smiled as he got to work. "Are you related to Jack Johnston?" I asked innocently.

He looked over his shoulder at me. "I was. But I suppose you've heard that he's dead now. I guess I'm not quite as related as I once was." He grinned.

The grin surprised me. "I'm so sorry for your loss. Were you close?"

He shook his head. "No, we weren't close. He was my nephew, but we had never been close to one another." He spat on the ground. "My brother died last year, and that about broke my heart. We were close. My brother was a good man. But that boy of his?" He shook his head. "No, ma'am, we weren't close."

"I'm sorry to hear that. It's tough when a family doesn't get along as well as they would like to."

He snorted and turned on the spray washer. "Jack was a good kid, but something happened when he got older. I guess life just kind of turns you sometimes. I'd hardly even call him my nephew, if you want to know the truth." He sprayed the front of my car, moving the hose quickly and expertly over every square inch.

"I'm so sorry," I said. "I'm sorry for the loss of your

brother, too. It can be very difficult to lose somebody you're close to."

He nodded but didn't say anything for a bit. He continued moving his hose over my car and moved around to the side of it. He was moving quickly, and I was pretty sure this wasn't going to take him long.

"Still, it can be really hard when a family member is murdered," I tried again. I needed him to open up to me if I was going to learn anything new.

He nodded. "Yeah, it sure was a shock to me. I don't know what he must have done to get himself murdered. But if you want to know the truth, he wasn't a nice guy, so I suppose anything could've happened. You know what he did to me?" He turned and looked at me, the water still spraying on my car.

I shook my head, hopeful that he was going to give me some valuable information now. "No, what?"

He released the water sprayer. "Cheated me out of my inheritance."

I shook my head. "What do you mean? How did he cheat you out of your inheritance?"

"My brother was supposed to give me two hundred and fifty thousand dollars in his will. He told me exactly how much he was going to give me. He made a lot of money in the stock market, and he told me exactly what he was going to give me." He spat on the ground again. "But Jack, he talked him out of it.

Told him some lies about me, and my brother changed his mind."

I shook my head. "Oh my gosh. Really?"

He nodded. "Really. I still can't get over it. I can't believe that my brother would listen to him and take his side of it. We had been close all our lives. He was my big brother, and he practically raised me because he was fifteen years older than me, and both our parents had to work to support us. When my parents died, they didn't have a penny to their name. They had a hard time raising me, but Andrew stepped in and was there for all of us. That makes people close, you know? When somebody does something that nice for you, that makes you close. He could've just wandered off and lived his own life without even thinking about me, but he didn't do that."

"It sounds like you two were very close."

He nodded again. "We sure were. He said he was going to take care of me when he died, and then he did die. Had a heart attack. I was shocked when I found out that the will had been changed. Nobody even told me it was changed until after he died. I was asking what was going on because I knew there was some monkey business afoot, and Jack told me his father never meant to leave me that much money. Can you believe that? I certainly couldn't, not after he told me exactly what he was going to leave me."

"That's awful," I said, nodding. "How did Jack get him to change the will?"

He shook his head. "He said I stole money from our mother and made her life miserable. Can you believe that?" He shook his head and spat again. "I still can't get over it. I can't believe that my brother would even believe something like that. I always helped look after our mother. She lived to be a hundred and four and Jack was still just a kid when she died. He wouldn't have known what was going on with her, but he told Andrew he saw me yell at her and demand money. He brings it up all these years later, see. It's just crazy to think that I would do anything to hurt her."

"That sounds like a mess. Did he leave you any money in his will?"

He nodded. "Oh sure, he left me ten thousand. Ten thousand is nothing. I was going to pay off all my equipment for my business with that money, but all I was able to do was pay off a couple of things. I need a brand-new truck. My truck is ten years old and has nearly two hundred thousand miles on it. I need something new, and I was going to buy a nice truck with that money, but the little I got didn't get me anywhere. I tell you, I'd like to feel sorry for Jack being murdered the way he was, but I don't. I don't feel bad at all."

"I can see where you would be angry at him. Nobody wants to be lied about, especially when it has to do with your own mother."

He nodded and turned the water back on, and resumed spraying the car. "You better believe it. If you ask me, he got what he deserved. Nobody goes around and lies on me like that. Repercussions are going to come."

"Repercussions?" *Was he admitting to the murder?*

He nodded. "The universe will take care of its own. I'm telling you right now, he got what he deserved because he was such an awful rascal. You don't do things like he did and not expect to have repercussions come."

I studied Hal as he continued washing my car. Those repercussions had to have come from *him*. "Hal, are you in Jack's will?" I had to ask. I had to know if he got any money out of Jack.

He snorted. "Oh, sure, if you call five thousand dollars being included in the will. The lawyer called me this morning. Jack had so much money that he inherited from his father, it's not even funny. Honestly, five thousand? That's a slap in the face."

Jack must have changed his mind and left him a token amount. I wondered how Merlene would feel about that when she found out.

74

"Who got the rest of his money?" I asked cautiously.

He shot me a look. "His wife and daughter, I guess. I tell you, the police ought to be looking at them and talking to them about that. That wife of his is so self-ish, it's not even funny. She made out like a bandit, and I'm pretty sure that if anybody wanted to kill him, it had to be her."

"Did he leave money to anybody else? Anybody outside of the family?" It wasn't a surprise that his wife got most of his money. That was the way that it should be, but I wondered if there was anybody else who made out like a bandit.

He shrugged. "I don't know. All I know is all I got was five thousand. I'm worth a whole lot more than that. But his wife is the greediest person you ever saw. Believe me, she would kill for money."

I studied Hal as he continued working. He was angry and bitter about the money. And anger and bitterness might lead to murder.

CHAPTER 10

J had already made up my mind as to who the killer was. It had to be Uncle Hal. Who else could it be? He was bitter about being cut out of his brother's will, and he blamed Jack. That was reason enough to kill him.

Alec had finally gotten some time off work, and we were headed over to the co-op to pick out pumpkins. I couldn't stand that fall had already begun, and we didn't have any pumpkins for the house.

"You know that Uncle Hal did it, right?" I said as he drove.

He shook his head without looking at me. "No, he didn't do it. He has an alibi."

My head whipped around to look at him. "What

are you talking about? He's the killer. He has the most motive to kill his nephew. It was over money."

He smiled. "Allie, he has an airtight alibi. He had an early morning breakfast date at Monroe's Café. More than a handful of people saw him, and his date said he had spent the previous night with her. In Ellsworth."

I gasped again. "Uncle Hal had a date?"

He chuckled, shaking his head. "Yes, Uncle Hal had a date. I've already talked to her as well as the people at Monroe's. He was far too occupied to have had time to kill him."

I groaned. "Why didn't you tell me this earlier? I swear, he has the most reason to do it."

He shook his head. "Nope. Not this time."

He pulled into the co-op, and we got out. I was mulling over what he just told me, but the sight of stacks and stacks of pumpkins just inside the co-op brightened my evening. "Oh, look at them. Look at all the beautiful pumpkins." I was almost giddy with excitement.

"Try to hold yourself back," he said wryly. "We don't need that many pumpkins."

I gasped and looked at him. "Those are fightin' words. There's no such thing as too many pumpkins."

He chuckled. "Believe me, there are." He picked up

a small shopping basket and put it over his arm. "You can have whatever fits into this basket."

I shook my head. "No way. That thing will only hold a handful of small pumpkins. I'm getting big ones."

He shook his head. "We don't need more than a few small ones."

I waved a dismissive hand at him and grabbed a shopping cart. I needed pumpkins of all sizes to decorate with. I pushed the shopping cart inside and headed straight over to the shelves where I sold jams and jellies and was surprised to see that I had nearly sold out of everything I had there. I usually checked on my inventory frequently, but it had been several weeks now. I was slacking.

"Well, what do we have here? Empty shelves?"

I glanced at Alec. "Oh, you. It won't take long to refill them. I'll make some apple butter and pumpkin butter and fill this right up. I can't wait. I love the smell of apple butter. Maybe I'll make some cranberry chutney, too."

"We've got to have the cranberry chutney."

I rolled my eyes at him and pushed the cart over to a cardboard box of large pumpkins. "I want two large pumpkins, one for either side of the fireplace in the living room."

He sighed. "You're going to get your way again, aren't you?"

"Did you doubt I would?"

He shook his head. "Nope."

I looked up and was surprised to see Bella Johnston headed in our direction. She was wearing a green apron that all the employees at the co-op wore. It really must have been a while since I'd been here because I had no idea that she worked here. I smiled at her. "Hi Bella, I didn't know you worked here."

She smiled and nodded. "I've been working here for a few weeks now, and I love it. I get to talk to lots of people, and we have a lot of cute fall and Halloween stuff that I'm going to spend most of my paycheck on."

"It's a great place," I said. "Bella, I am so sorry to hear about your father."

She nodded, frowning now. "Thank you. It was kind of a shock to find out about him." She looked at Alec. "Hello, Detective. Do you have my father's killer in custody yet?"

Alec shook his head. "Not yet, but I'm sure it will be soon."

She frowned again. "Really? You're really that close to arresting someone? I was hoping you would have already done that, but I guess if it will be soon, I can't complain."

He narrowed his eyes at her slightly. "Let's just say that I'm working diligently on the case and doing everything I can to get the killer arrested."

She nodded, taking this in. "I just hope that you get the killer behind bars soon. They have no right to be walking this earth freely when my father is dead. I still can't get over it. I can't believe somebody killed him." She glanced at me.

"It's just terrible," I said. "I talked to your mother the other day, and she was so upset. Your grandmother, too."

She nodded. "We're all beside ourselves." She sighed, shaking her head. "Just beside ourselves with grief. I just don't understand who would be so horrible as to kill him. Actually, I take that back. I know who killed him. It was my great Uncle Hal. He's a horrible, awful man, and he and my father argued just days before he died."

"Oh?" I said. "What did they fight over?" Alec may have said that Hal had an alibi, but maybe he got people to lie for him. As far as I was concerned, he was my top suspect.

She sighed. "Money. Can you believe that? That old man came over to our house and demanded that my father give him more money. My father told him he wasn't going to get any more, but he felt like he was supposed to get money from my grandfather's death. I guess he didn't leave him much, and that's his fault. He wasn't nice to my grandfather. He fought with him too."

"Really?" I said. "So they had a lot of issues too?"

She nodded. "Oh, yes. It's well known that Uncle Hal can't get along with anyone. He's a horrible man. Plus, I know that he owns guns. I've seen them hanging on the wall in his house. It wouldn't surprise me one bit if he killed my father. My mom said the same thing. She's sure that he has to be the killer, too."

Alec looked at her. "He has an alibi."

Her eyes widened. "What are you talking about? What do you mean? He has to be the killer. There's nobody else who would want to kill my father."

He shrugged. "He has an alibi. He is no longer a person of interest."

She took this in. "Well, who else do you think would have killed him? I swear to you, there's no one else that would want him dead like that." She tucked her blond hair back behind her ear, revealing diamond stud earrings.

"I'm still talking to people. Don't worry, I will figure out who killed your father." I sensed a bit of annoyance in Alec now.

Bella squirmed. "Well, I can't imagine who else you would be looking at. Who are you talking to?

Who is it that you think killed my father? I have a right to know."

Alec shook his head. "No, you don't have a right to know. And I'd rather keep that information to myself for now. But you don't have anything to worry about."

She huffed, her hands on her hips. "Of course I have a right to know. He's my father. I have a right to know what's going on with the investigation into his murder. I want to know who you're talking to."

Alec's brow furrowed. "I assure you, Bella, I'm working diligently on this case, and I will find the killer. Are you sure there's nobody else that may have had a reason to kill him?"

She hesitated. "The only other person I can think of that might have wanted him dead was my Aunt Lynn. She also felt like she didn't get enough money from my grandfather's death. Can you believe that? My grandmother got most of the money, as she should have, and then the rest was divided among the family the way he saw fit, but neither Uncle Hal nor Aunt Lynn was happy about it. My dad always said they were greedy."

"Did you get money in the will?" I asked.

She took a deep breath and shook her head. "No. None of the grandkids got any money, it went to our parents. My grandfather thought they should disperse it as they saw fit. And that is completely understandable."

I nodded. "That sounds about right. It was nice that he had money to take care of his family when he was gone."

She nodded. "My grandfather had a lot of money. I know that my grandmother is very well taken care of and will be until she dies. Then the rest of that money will probably be passed down to the grandkids since their kids got their share already. I have three cousins to share it with."

"That's nice for all of you."

I wondered about all of this. It seemed that this family was very concerned about the money and where it was going. And now, we needed to talk to Aunt Lynn to see what she had to say about it.

She smiled. "Well, I better get back to work. These pumpkins aren't going to sell themselves." She glanced at the piles of pumpkins sitting about the co-op.

"I'm so glad y'all got so many of them in this year. You can bet that I'm going to pick out more than my fair share."

"You can say that again," Alec said.

She nodded. "I'll talk to you later." And she was gone.

When she was out of earshot, I turned to Alec. "What do you make of that?"

He sighed. "I'm not going to tell her every detail about the case, that's for sure."

"That was kind of pushy of her."

He grinned. "And she sure was set on Uncle Hal being the killer. Must be a disappointment to find out that he didn't do it."

I nodded. "I'm rather disappointed myself. Can you pick up this big pumpkin and put it in my shopping cart?"

He looked at the one I indicated and scowled. "That pumpkin is far too large to put into the shopping cart."

"It's alright. You'll manage."

As much as I hated to let go of the idea that Hal was the killer—if Alec was certain he couldn't have done it—then I needed to put my efforts into looking at someone else.

CHAPTER 11

*D*ixie entwined himself around my legs as I washed the dishes. I'd been baking up a storm, having received a dozen orders for cinnamon rolls so far. I had no idea they would be as popular as they were, and I was pleased as punch. But that meant a lot of dirty dishes, and I was spending the morning catching up, cleaning my pans, utensils, and large bowls. Lucy and I had skipped our morning run, having already put in more miles in a week than we normally did. Sometimes you just needed to take the day off, and I was enjoying my coffee and a cinnamon roll, and now I needed to do a little cleaning around the house or Alec was going to wonder if I had abandoned him.

"Dixie, don't you have something else to do? I'm

going to trip over you if you're not careful." Dixie was an attention grabber. If you didn't give him your attention, he would grab it from you. Unless he was in the mood to spend time by himself. Since we had moved to this house, he spent a lot of time on the patio, where I had planted loads of flowers and flowering bushes. There was also a large water fountain Alec had put in for me, and he loved to jump up and balance himself along the ledge, drinking the fresh running water. It was a cat's paradise.

The chiming doorbell startled me, and I jumped, nearly dropping the large yellow bowl I used to let the cinnamon roll dough rise in. "I wonder who that could be," I muttered to myself, as I put the bowl back into the sink and rinsed the soap from my hands. There was another chime of the doorbell before I could even get my hands dried. "Well, Dixie, they appear to be in some sort of hurry." I headed to the front door before they could hit the doorbell a third time.

I was surprised when I saw who was at the door. Lynn Johnston; Jack's sister. I smiled. "Oh, good morning, Lynn."

She forced herself to smile, but she looked flustered. "Good morning, Allie. I'm so sorry to bother you here at your home, but I wondered if I could speak with you for a few moments."

I nodded. "Oh, of course. Come on in. I've made some fresh cinnamon rolls, and I've got coffee ready. Would you like some?"

She nodded and followed me into the kitchen. "That sounds really good. I hate to be a bother to you."

"Oh, it's no bother," I said, as I got cups and plates out and set them on the table. "I'm working on my cinnamon roll recipe, so you're in luck. Freshly made cinnamon rolls." I brought a plate with the cinnamon rolls on it to the table. "Help yourself."

"Oh, Allie, those are beautiful. You made them?"

I poured coffee into the cups. "I sure did. I think this is one of my favorite recipes. I love cinnamon so much. Your mother asked me to make some for the meal after the funeral."

She nodded and took a fork, spearing a roll, and put it on one of the small plates. "I love cinnamon too. It's one of my favorite flavors and favorite scents." She licked her lips, then looked up at me. I could tell she was working up the nerve to say something, and I wondered what it could be. I hoped it was something that would help us find her brother's killer.

"I'm so sorry about Jack," I said. "It was a shock to find out about what happened to him." I didn't know if she knew that Lucy and I had found his body, and I wasn't going to tell her if she didn't already know.

She nodded without looking at me now. "It's horrible. It's just unfathomable that somebody would do something like that to him. I don't understand it." I could hear the emotion in her voice, and my heart went out to her. "My poor mother is heartbroken."

"I'm so sorry. I don't know what I would do if something like that happened to my family. Your mother is going to need your support now more than ever." I pushed the creamer and one of the cups of coffee toward her, and she helped herself to them. I sat down across from her.

She frowned. "Mother isn't speaking to me. She gets in one of her moods, and won't speak to me for weeks."

"Oh. I'm sorry." The more I heard about this family, the more it didn't surprise me that someone had ended up dead. They had issues.

She nodded. "She'll come around. She always does."

I smiled. "So what's going on, Lynn? Is there something I can help you with?"

She licked her lower lip, looked up at me, and then took a quick sip of her coffee. "I don't know. I mean, I know Alec is working on the case, and I am desperate to find out who murdered my brother. But I don't know if there's anything that you can do. But I just had to come and see you and talk to you about this."

I nodded and took a sip of my coffee. "It's good just to have somebody to talk to about difficult things. Sometimes people who are closer to you aren't the people you want to discuss them with." I watched her as I spoke. Lynn was a troubled woman.

She nodded and looked at me again. "It's about Merlene, Jack's wife." She hesitated with her mouth open as she tried to come up with what she wanted to say. She nodded again. "I think she killed my brother."

"Oh, my," I said. "Why do you think that?"

She inhaled and cut into the cinnamon roll with the edge of the fork. "It's just that, well, things weren't good between the two of them before my brother died." She glanced at me and then returned to the cinnamon roll, shoving a small piece into her mouth.

"I see," I said carefully. "So they were fighting a lot?"

"A lot. I'm pretty sure they were on the verge of divorce. My brother would sometimes let things slip. He said there were issues, and they had tried counseling last year, but apparently, nothing came of it. And not only that but Merlene—she's changed." She looked at me meaningfully.

"Changed how?" I felt like we were on the verge of something here. Lynn was clearly upset about things going on between her brother and his wife, and now that he had been murdered, maybe she was connecting dots that she hadn't quite connected before.

She swallowed, then took a sip of her coffee. "Have you seen her lately?"

I nodded. "Yes, I saw her a few days ago."

"Have you seen what she's done to herself? She's lost weight and changed her hairstyle and color. And the makeup. I swear, it's like she suddenly learned how to do her makeup and well, she just looks different. Younger." She looked at me meaningfully again.

I knew she wanted me to connect my own dots, but I wanted her to tell me exactly what she thought was going on. "Yes, she did look very nice when I spoke to her." I waited for her to continue.

She took a deep breath. "Yes, she looks nice. She looks very, very nice. Like she put herself through her own change of life program. She lost weight, she made all those changes to her outward appearance, and she's been spending money. Lots and lots of money. Designer clothes, designer handbags, and shoes. And it upset Jack terribly. He thought she was having an affair, and he accused her of it, but of course, she denied it. I told him he was crazy to think that Merlene would do something like that. It just wasn't something she would do. Now that Jack has been murdered, I think he was right. I wish I had believed him when he told me, but I just couldn't see Merlene doing that. But now I can."

I nodded slowly. "Do you have any proof that she may have been having an affair?"

She sighed and shook her head. "No, I don't have any proof. Honestly, I wouldn't have even thought about it, except that Jack told me that, and now that he's been murdered, I believe she wanted to get rid of him. Look at all the money she stood to inherit if he died. There was a lot of money. Our father left him the bulk of his inheritance, expecting him to manage it and leave it for the rest of the family members if he should die. I thought that was ridiculous, but there was no talking sense into my father at times." She snorted angrily, shaking her head.

I could feel the bitterness rolling off her. "Your father didn't leave you any money?"

She shook her head. "Oh, no, he left me money. It's just that he left the bulk of it to my brother. I mean, he was only seven years older than me. So why would he leave him all the money? By bulk, I mean that he did give me some money, but it didn't make any sense to me not to divide it up equally. But Jack was always his favorite." Her cheeks were pink now, and she was gripping the coffee cup in her hands.

"How much money did he leave you? Do you mind me asking?"

She shook her head. "One hundred thousand. That's nothing to sneeze at, but you have to understand that he left my brother a million dollars. And half of that money belongs to me. But now it's going to Merlene."

"What about your mother? How much money did he leave her?"

She sighed. "My mother received over three million. The bulk of it went to her, I guess, and not my brother, but the money that was to go to the two of us kids, he got the bulk of that money. I don't know. Maybe I'm expecting too much, but it was wrong of my father to do that. He had no business giving all that money to him. I told Jack he needed to give me my share now, but he refused to do it."

I gazed at Lynn. Her father had caused a lot of trouble in this family by not being equitable with the money that he left as an inheritance. That trouble may have led to his son's death.

"I think it would be good to speak to Alec about this, about your suspicions of Merlene, I mean. If she's having an affair, it would be good for him to know."

She nodded. "You're right. I should just talk to Alec. But I swear Merlene has to be behind his murder. Now she can go off with all her money and enjoy her life without any issues from her husband."

I nodded, taking this in. It was an interesting twist. If Merlene had been planning on murdering him so she could get away with all the money, then she may have done just that. It was something that I was going to look into.

CHAPTER 12

*I*t wasn't thirty minutes after Lynn left when there was another knock on my door. I had been mulling over what she told me about Merlene, and I couldn't help but wonder if she might be his killer.

"I wonder who that could be?" I mused, rising from the kitchen table. I had just finished washing the morning dishes, and another batch of cinnamon rolls was in the oven.

I wiped my hands on a dish towel and headed to the door.

"Oh!" I exclaimed when I opened my door.

Margaret Johnston smiled at me from the front step. "Good morning, Allie. I hope I'm not disturbing you."

I shook my head and returned her smile. "No, not at all. How are you doing, Margaret?"

She shrugged. "I guess I'm doing about as well as can be expected. Still trying to make myself understand that my son is dead." Her bottom lip trembled when she said it, but she quickly recovered and smiled again.

I shook my head. "I'm so sorry. This must be so hard for you. Would you like to come in? I'm baking fresh cinnamon rolls, and I've got coffee ready."

"I would love to."

I ushered her into the kitchen and fetched fresh coffee cups and plates. I had never had two visitors to my home on the same day, especially two unexpected visitors who were related to a murder victim, but I wasn't about to complain. The more information I could gather, the better.

"I'll get that cinnamon roll and coffee for you."

She nodded and sat at the table. "That would be wonderful. Allie, you bake the best cinnamon rolls I've ever tasted. I'm a fairly good baker myself, but I don't think I can bake a cinnamon roll half as well as you can."

I smiled at her praise, but I was a bit suspicious as to why she was lavishing it so generously. "Oh, Margaret, you're flattering me. But I do like to hear that someone appreciates my baking."

"I'm not flattering you. I mean it. They're simply the best cinnamon rolls that I've ever eaten."

"Thank you," I said, filling two cups with coffee and setting out two cinnamon rolls. I wasn't sure I could eat another cinnamon roll since I just finished one when Lynn was here, but I was going to do my best.

"What brings you out this way, Margaret?"

She took a sip of her coffee before answering. "I don't know. I guess I was a bit lonely, and it was so kind of you to bring those cinnamon rolls by the other day. In fact, I was thinking I would like to place an order for three dozen cinnamon rolls for the meal after Jack's funeral, if you have the time."

I nodded. "Of course I have the time. I'll even make them for free. They'll be my donation."

Her eyes widened. "Oh, are you sure? You don't have to do that. I would gladly pay you for them."

I shook my head. "It would be my honor to make them for you. I'll get them baked and drop them by your house early in the morning. Was the funeral Saturday?" I had seen the obituary in the paper and the funeral was pushed back further than I had imagined it would be.

She nodded. "Yes, Saturday at eleven a.m."

"How about I bring them by around 7:30? Is that too early?"

She shook her head. "I expect I won't be getting much sleep. I'll be up."

My heart truly went out to her. I couldn't imagine enduring what she was going through now. "I'll make sure I get them to you on time." I waited to see if she wanted to talk about anything else.

She nodded and cut into her cinnamon roll with her fork. "This is really quite wonderful, Allie," she said, without looking at me. "Is your husband close to finding my son's killer?" She looked up at me now, and there was such sadness in her eyes.

"Well, he's been spending a lot of time working on the case. I don't know if he's ready to make an arrest, but I can tell you he's putting everything into this that he's got."

She nodded again. "I respect your husband very much. I know that he takes his job seriously, and I appreciate that. To be honest, I've been thinking things over, and I'm wondering about Jack's Uncle Hal. The two didn't get along, you know."

I wasn't sure what was going on here, but everybody in that family seemed to blame the murder on Uncle Hal. I had finally dismissed him as a suspect since Alec had, but apparently, the memo had not been sent out to the rest of the family.

"I see," I said. "But do you think there's anybody else who could have done it?"

She shook her head. "No. I really don't. His daughter absolutely adored her father, you know. She was a daddy's girl and always will be. He doted on her. She's a difficult girl. A real handful. But she loved her father." She took another bite of the cinnamon roll and nodded appreciatively. "Excellent as usual."

"Thank you. How was his relationship with his wife?"

She looked up at me. "His wife? Well, I suppose they were like any other married couple. They had their moments where they didn't get along, but Merlene tried to be a very good wife to him, and he tried to be a good husband to her." She smiled. "They made the sweetest couple."

I nodded. "So, there were no issues going on with them?" Was Lynn making things up?

She hesitated. "Well, I did notice that Merlene sort of spruced herself up recently." She chuckled. "I suppose that's not a term one would use to talk about someone who's made improvements to themselves, but that's what she has done. She's made lots of improvements to herself. And to the house. She bought new furniture and had some remodeling done when they got the money from my husband's death. I can't blame them for it. Their house was so dated, and they were having some electrical issues that needed to be addressed. Why? Has your husband said something about her?"

I shook my head. "No, he hasn't said anything. I was just wondering, is all. I've been thinking about the different relationships Jack had."

Alec did have his eye on Merlene, but he still couldn't find anything specific that suggested she was the killer. So for now, he was just keeping her in mind. But I wasn't going to tell Margaret that.

She nodded. "It just breaks my heart. Both she and my granddaughter are without the leader of their family. He was such a good husband and father. He was always involved in their lives, and he did his best to make good decisions for the family. Merlene left most of the big decisions to him, you know. That's how much confidence she had in his ability to lead the family. And poor Bella is just beside herself now that her father is gone. I worry about her. She's still so young, and I hate to think she might fall under the influence of somebody who wasn't as upstanding as her father was."

"Oh?" I asked, taking a sip of my coffee. "Has somebody come into her life recently that isn't a good influence on her?"

She hesitated. "She has a new boyfriend. He's, well, a ruffian." She chuckled. "That's what I call him. My son said that I was being silly, but I'm not being silly.

There's something about him that I don't like. He's coarse and uses foul language. I don't like a man like that."

I nodded. "I know what you mean. There's no reason to use language like that." I leaned forward, hoping she would give me more information. I would agree to anything she said right now if she could give me the information that I needed to know about who killed her son. "Has he done anything specific to worry you?"

She frowned. "He dropped out of college and doesn't have a very good job. From the looks of it, he has no intention of going back to school or looking for a better job. I told her that's no life for her. She shouldn't have to spend her life supporting a man."

"I see."

She sighed. "I suppose there's no use worrying myself over things like that. She's an adult now, and she is capable of making up her own mind about how she wants to live her life. But I don't like him. Not one bit."

"What's his name?" I asked and took a bite of my cinnamon roll.

"Damon Reed. He works down at the garage. He's not a mechanic. I think he just does odds and ends around the shop. That's another thing. If he were a mechanic, that would be a respectable job, but I get the feeling that he doesn't do much other than clean up or fetch tools for the mechanics. I don't know. I just don't like him." She shook her head and took another bite of her cinnamon roll.

"I know who Damon Reed is," I said. "I've met him a couple of times when I took my car down to the garage. He was polite, but I guess that's really about all that I know about him." I made a mental note to add Damon to my list of people to talk to. If he was making Margaret this uncomfortable then I wondered if he was up to something. Like murder.

CHAPTER 13

*M*y car was almost due for an oil change, so I decided to drop by the garage to see if Damon Reed was there. My impression of him was that he was quiet and kept to himself, diligently doing his job. Of course, I didn't know him well, so that may not have been the case at all. I wanted to see if he had anything to say about Jack's murder.

On the way over, I picked Lucy up. It was always good to have reinforcements.

"So, both Jack's mother and sister stopped by to see you today?" she asked when I told her about the visits.

I nodded. "It seemed kind of strange to me. I think they wanted to see if I had any information about what was going on in the investigation and they didn't want to go straight to Alec."

"Because they thought they could get more out of you," she said. "Alec would be businesslike with them and wouldn't tell them certain things."

I nodded. "I'm making three dozen cinnamon rolls for Saturday for the funeral. I told her I would make them for free."

She nodded. "That's nice of you. I'm sure she appreciates it. But why would she be so interested in what's going on with the investigation? Other than the official version, she would have gotten from Alec. Because he would keep the family up-to-date about what was going on. It almost sounds like she wanted to know if you knew something that wasn't so official."

"That's exactly what I think. And it makes me wonder if she's not telling everything she knows." I didn't want to think ill of her since she had just lost her son, but I had to wonder. Both she and her daughter came to talk to me about the murder on the same day. That was some kind of crazy coincidence.

I parked in front of the garage, and we walked into the office. I was surprised to see that there weren't any other customers. That was good. It would allow us to talk to him privately. It was mid-afternoon, and I hoped he was at work.

There was a small silver bell on the front counter, and the counter was strewn with work orders and car magazines. We turned to look at the rest of the office. The smell of grease hung in the air, and a coffee pot sat on the corner table. Personally, I wouldn't have attempted to drink the coffee from that pot because there were grease smudges on the outside of it.

"We're not drinking that coffee," Lucy said.

"No, we are not."

"Oh! Can I help you ladies?" someone said from behind us. I turned around and was pleased to see Damon Reed. He was wiping his hands on a red rag. "I didn't hear you ladies come in."

I smiled. "Yes, I was hoping y'all had time to change the oil in my car. I suppose I should have made an appointment, but I was out running errands and I decided to just drop by and see if you had the time."

He looked behind him into the garage and turned back and nodded. "Yeah, I think we've got time if you've got a few minutes to wait."

I nodded. "Sure. We've got time." We sat down on the stools in front of the counter, and he searched for a blank work order in the mess on the desk.

"You've been in here before, haven't you? I think I recognize you."

I nodded. "Yes, Allie Blanchard."

He started typing into the computer. "Here it is. Let me fill out this work order for you, and we'll get you started."

"I expected you to be much busier today," Lucy said, looking around the office.

He nodded. "We had a few other appointments, but a couple of them were canceled. You picked a good day to bring your car in for an oil change."

"Oh, that's fantastic," I said. "Aren't you dating Bella Johnston? I thought I saw the two of you out at dinner not long ago." It was a lie.

He looked up at me, surprised. "Yeah, we've been dating for a few months. Where did you see us?"

I thought about it for a moment and then shook my head. "I can't seem to remember. I just remembered you from here at the garage because you were so polite the last couple of times I was in, and Bella Johnston is always so sweet when I go into the co-op."

He smiled and nodded. "Yeah, you must've hit her on a good day." He chuckled. "No, I'm just kidding. Bella is a sweet girl."

Damon was tall and blond, with a grease smudge on his chin. He seemed nice enough and I wondered what it was that bothered Margaret about him.

"It's a shame that her father died recently," Lucy said sadly. "The poor girl must be having a tough time with it."

He nodded. "Yeah, it's been rough on her. It's been rough for both of us, to be honest because she's so sad all the time now." His smirk and tone of voice made me think that neither of them was struggling with the death.

"I just can't imagine losing a parent so young. Especially since it was her father. I heard that she was very close to her father," I said.

He stopped typing on the computer and looked at me. "Where did you hear that?"

I smiled. "From her grandmother. The poor thing. She's so sad and broken up over the death of her son. His death has left a tremendous hole in that family."

He nodded somberly. "Yeah, I suppose so. But between the three of us, Bella wasn't that close to her father. He wasn't a nice guy, to be honest. I guess I can see where his mother would think he was because mothers always want to think the best of their sons. But he was kind of a jerk to Bella."

"Oh, really?" I asked. "I didn't know that. What a shame. But still, that was her father, and she has to be grieving terribly for him."

He shrugged and placed the purchase order on the clipboard, filling it out with my name and address.

"Yeah, I guess so. It's funny that he was killed out in the middle of nowhere." He smiled now and kept writing.

Lucy and I glanced at each other. "Funny? What do you mean by 'funny'?" Lucy asked.

He shrugged. "Out there on that old road? People are out there exercising now and then, and the last thing he would've been doing was any kind of exercise or anything else that would have been good for him. He was just that kind of person. He worked a lot and didn't have much to do with his family."

I studied him. I could see why Margaret wasn't enthusiastic about him dating her granddaughter. Now that I'd had a few minutes to talk to him, I could see he was the one who was kind of a jerk. "I heard they were a very close family."

He snorted. "Yeah, I guess."

"Do you have any idea who might have wanted to kill Jack?" I asked. I figured there was no harm in just coming out and asking him the question.

He looked up at me, still smiling. I wanted to wipe it right off his face. "Yeah, his wife. She's got a boyfriend, you know. Jack didn't want to believe that, but I know that she does."

Now we were getting somewhere. "What do you mean you know she had a boyfriend? Who is it?"

He shook his head and turned back to the computer. "Oh, I don't have a name or anything. But no woman fixes herself up like that and then doesn't have a boyfriend. She wasn't doing it for her husband. I can tell you that much."

"How do you know that?" Lucy said. "There's no harm in making yourself as attractive as you can for your husband."

He chuckled. "Yeah, but she wasn't doing it for him. Trust me. She's buying designer clothes, designer handbags, and jewelry. A man buys those things for his wife. She doesn't buy it for herself unless she's buying it because she wants to impress someone."

I was stunned. Stunned because this guy didn't appear to be the kind of person who noticed details like that, but also stunned because he was right. A man buys his wife those kinds of things, and if the wife has to buy them herself, she was buying them for somebody else.

"Did you ever see her out with anyone? Did she ever hint that she was going out with somebody else?"

He shook his head. "No, I never saw her with anyone. And she sure wasn't going to be dropping any hints. She didn't want anybody to know about that. If she messed up her marriage, she might be kicked out of the will. And her old man had a lot of money. Trust me. But think about it. If she bumps him off, she gets everything. She's his wife. Everything goes to her."

"If he had a will, he could leave some of the money to other people, though," Lucy said. "His wife could contest the will, I suppose, but he can still name other people."

He nodded. "Yeah, maybe so, but Bella told me that the bulk of the money went to her mother. And she isn't wasting any time spending it, either. She just bought a fancy car two days ago. It's a really nice one. I wish I had one like that. But I don't know if I'll ever have the money to be able to buy something like that."

I gazed at him. He was much more observant than I would have given him credit for.

And Alec needed to talk to Merlene again. Lucy and I might drop in on her ourselves.

CHAPTER 14

"I don't like that Damon Reed."

I nodded and knocked on Alec's office door with the toe of my boot. My hands held pumpkin spice lattes, and a small bakery box of cinnamon rolls was tucked beneath my arm. "There's something about him that I don't like either. I can't quite put my finger on it. Maybe it was his smug smirk or that self-assured smile." I shook my head and knocked again.

Moments later, Alec opened the door and grinned when he saw us. "Well, lookie here. What are you two up to?"

I held up the pumpkin spice lattes. "I thought my husband could use some afternoon refreshment, so we stopped by the Cup and Bean and got some pumpkin spice lattes. Then, I ran by the house and picked up some cinnamon rolls. Do you have a few minutes?"

"For you? Always." He leaned over and kissed me. "Hey, Lucy."

He stepped back, and we walked into his office.

"Hi, Alec. Allie, I think he means he always has time for a pumpkin spice latte and your cinnamon rolls," Lucy said, as we sat down in front of his desk.

"I think so too," I agreed.

He grinned and sat in his chair. "Oh, that's not fair. I love seeing my beautiful wife and her lovely friend."

I chuckled and set the coffee on the desk, then put the bakery box next to it. "I've had about all the cinnamon rolls I can handle today. My two visitors each got one, and it would have been rude not to eat one with them."

"Two visitors?" he asked suspiciously and took a sip of his coffee. He nodded appreciatively. "Very tasty."

I filled him in on my talk with Margaret and Lynn, and then our visit to the local garage. "I wonder if something's going on that made both ladies stop by the house today. I mean, it couldn't be a coincidence, could it?"

He sat back in his chair and took another sip of

his coffee. "Maybe. Maybe not. Maybe they've been comparing notes, and they each wanted to make it look like they came up with it on their own."

"Then why would they both come on the same day?" Lucy asked.

He shrugged. "Maybe they didn't realize that the other one was going to drop by the same day. It would have been fun if they had run into one another."

I nodded. "Yes, if Margaret was already inside the house, and then Lynn came to the door, and they were intending to not let on that they each planned to drop by. It would have been fun." I didn't know if this was what was going on or not. It really could have been just a coincidence, but it made me wonder. "Anything new on the case?"

He sighed. "Not enough to make an arrest."

"I still wonder why Jack was out there where we found him," Lucy said. "And that newspaper. It had to mean something, didn't it?"

"Can I borrow the newspaper? I need to read it," I said. There was nothing in the copy I got from Mr. Winters, so if it was significant, it had to be because Jack or someone else had made notes in it.

He chuckled. "No, I cannot give you that newspaper. You know it's evidence."

"Did they ever get any fingerprints off of it?"

He nodded. "Yes. There were several sets of faint fingerprints on the paper, and we have run them through the system."

"Who do they belong to?" I asked, taking a sip of my coffee.

He sighed, thinking about it for a moment. "The victim, the victim's wife, the victim's daughter, and the victim's daughter's boyfriend. But before you say anything, the boyfriend has an early morning job delivering newspapers. So his fingerprints are going to be on it."

"Oh," I said disappointedly. "And everybody else lives in the household, and they could have handed it off to one another. I just don't get why that newspaper was in his hands like that. It's odd."

"Maybe the killer has a sense of humor, and they were just setting him up in a weird way," Lucy said.

I shook my head. "I don't think so. The newspaper came from the house. So it has to be one of those three people who killed him."

"Except that his wife says he always took the newspaper with him to read at the park in the mornings."

I frowned. "What park?"

"The municipal park. Apparently, it's a part of his morning routine before he goes into the office. He grabs a cup of coffee and sits and reads the newspaper. He works in the office complex just across the street from the park."

I groaned. "So he probably had the newspaper with him when he was grabbed."

He nodded. "My thoughts exactly."

I shook my head. "There has to be an answer. Somebody has got to mess up and let it slip that they are the killer."

There was a knock at the door, and I jumped.

Alec chuckled and got up to answer the door. "Good afternoon, Lynn," he said. "Can I help you?"

"Yes, can I come in, please?"

Alec glanced over his shoulder. "Well, I have a couple of visitors right now, but you're more than welcome to come in."

Lynn smiled when she saw us, and Alec pulled a chair from the corner of the room for her to sit down. "Fancy running into you again, Allie."

"Right? Are we going to be in the way?" I asked her.

She shook her head. "No, you're fine." She turned to Alec. "I suppose you already know that I went to talk to Allie earlier. But so many things have been running through my mind, and I had to come talk to you."

"Of course," Alec said, sitting down. "What can I do for you?"

She nodded and crossed her legs. Lynn was in her late 40s or early 50s, and her straight blond hair was pulled back in a chignon. She was more dressed up than she had been when I saw her earlier.

"I just know that my sister-in-law did it. She killed my brother. That's the only thing that makes any sense. She had the most access to him, and they weren't getting along. They had gone to therapy last year. He told me their marriage was falling apart, and that she wanted to leave him. He begged her not to go and told her he would do anything that she wanted if she would just stay."

"Just because they were having problems doesn't mean she killed him," Alec pointed out.

She nodded. "I know, but it was like she had reinvented herself. It's not just that she changed the way she looked and dressed, it was more than that. It was the way she spoke."

"What do you mean?" he asked.

She sighed. "If you listen to her, it's like she's changed her accent. She always had a thick Maine accent. In fact, some words were hard even for me to understand. But if you listen now, she speaks very plainly, very clearly, and how should I put it? More sophisticated. It's like this weird act that she puts on now. But it's always there. It's not just at certain times."

My eyes widened. "Oh my gosh. You're right. I thought there was something odd about her, and I just kind of chalked it up to the change in her appearance. But you're right, she's changed the way she speaks. Almost like she took diction lessons."

"That is weird," Lucy said. "Who does that? Especially at her age?"

She nodded. "Exactly. She's not the same person she used to be. I think it had Jack so worried that he didn't even tell me about it. And believe me, he told me a lot, but I really feel now that he didn't tell me half of what was going on with her. I bet he knew there was another man. I bet he knew exactly who that man was, too."

"But you don't know who that man is?" Alec asked.

She shook her head. "No, I'm afraid I don't. To be honest, I don't even have proof that she is seeing someone else. It's a hunch. A very strong hunch."

"She certainly has changed quite a bit," Lucy agreed. "But why wouldn't she just divorce him? Why kill him?"

She shook her head. "The money. Our father had a lot of money. Millions. And he got control of the lion's share. It was put into a trust, and the money to support our mother is taken out of that. The rest he pretty much had free rein with."

"What about his daughter?" I asked. "How was his relationship with her?"

She hesitated. "For the most part they had a good relationship. Bella is a little spoiled, but that happens sometimes with only children. But Jack loved his daughter very much. He bragged on her all the time."

That contradicted what Damon had said. He said that Jack didn't have much to do with Bella.

"I'll have another talk with Merlene," Alec said. "But right now, we don't have any proof that she was seeing anyone. And to be honest, she seems sincere in her love for her husband."

She rolled her eyes. "She may seem sincere, but she's anything but. I do appreciate you digging into this further. I didn't mean to disturb you. I'll be going." She stood up.

"Thanks for stopping by," Alec said and saw her to the door.

Right now, my money was on Merlene. If she had a boyfriend, it would have benefited her to get rid of her husband so they could be free to be together.

CHAPTER 15

$\mathscr{A}$fter our morning run, Lucy and I decided to stop by the Cup and Bean Coffee Shop. I wanted to catch up with Mr. Winters and see if he had found out anything that would help with the case.

"Pumpkin spice?" Lucy asked as we stepped up to the counter.

I nodded. "Pumpkin spice." With fall comes that delectable beverage known as pumpkin spice latte. I couldn't pass it up.

The barista turned from what she was doing at the espresso machine and smiled. "Oh, good morning, ladies. Pumpkin spice?"

We chuckled. When the barista at the local coffee shop knows exactly what you're going to order before you say it, you know you've made that place your second home.

I nodded. "Yes, please. We would both like a medium pumpkin spice latte."

"Maybe with a little extra pumpkin spice," Lucy said. "I can't get enough of my favorite drink."

"You got it," she said, and she went to work on our drinks.

Lucy leaned over and looked into the bakery case, shaking her head. "I've been eating too many cinnamon rolls. I had better not."

I chuckled. "I know what you mean. I thought I would be tired of them by now, but I'm not."

I paid for our drinks, and we hurried over to Mr. Winters' table. His glasses were perched at the end of his nose, and he was engrossed in reading his newspaper.

I cleared my throat when we sat down. "Good morning, Mr. Winters."

He looked up. "Oh, good morning, ladies. How have you been? And where have you been? I expected to see you sooner than this."

I felt a little guilty then. We really should have checked in with him sooner. "I know, I'm sorry. We got busy and haven't been able to stop in until now."

"No, but you can whiz through the drive thru like

a race car driver. What have you found out about the case?"

Lucy and I glanced at each other.

"A lot of people were angry at the victim because he inherited a lot of money. So many people allow money to change the way they view others. I'll never understand it." Lucy shook her head.

He nodded and took a sip of his black coffee. "It's amazing, isn't it? Money makes the world go round, and it can get people killed, too."

I glanced under the table, but Sadie wasn't there.

"Where is Sadie? Is she all right?" I suddenly wondered if the darling little dog wasn't feeling well. She was getting up there in years, and I hoped she was all right.

He nodded. "I've got a few things to do after stopping here, and I didn't want to run back by the house and drop her off. She's taking a nap at home."

I nodded. "Good. I'm glad to hear it. So what have you got for us? Have you found out anything about the murder?" I took a sip of my coffee, and it was just as tasty and delightful as I had anticipated.

"Well," he said, leaning forward, "it would appear that our murder victim had a girlfriend on the side."

Lucy and I gasped.

"Really?" Lucy said. "Who?"

He took another sip of his coffee before answering. "Jeanette Hawkins." He paused, allowing it to sink in.

"Jeanette Hawkins?" I asked. "She works at the county library, doesn't she?"

He nodded. "She does. And she's a good fifteen years younger than Jack, if I had to take a guess."

"I think that's a good guess," Lucy said. "She does look like she's a bit younger than he was. But are you sure about this? She doesn't appear to be the sort of person who would go out with somebody like him. Not to speak ill of the dead."

His brow furrowed. "What are you trying to infer, Lucy?"

She shrugged. "I'm not trying to infer anything. She's pretty. And she's very sweet and talkative, and I just cannot imagine her having an affair with somebody like him. Not that there's anything wrong with him. He seemed like a nice person. But it just doesn't fit together with the image I have of either of them." She turned to me for my opinion.

I nodded. "I'm with Lucy. I wouldn't imagine the two of them being a couple."

He shrugged. "I have it on good authority that they were. They had been seeing each other for nearly a year."

I sighed, thinking about what this meant, given

what we already knew about the case. "Did your source say whether his wife knew about Jeanette?"

He shook his head. "He didn't know for sure, but this is a small town. If the affair was going on for nearly a year, I can imagine that somebody let it slip to her."

Lucy nodded. "If somebody knew about the affair, and it got spread around and got back to his wife, that might make her angry enough to kill him. I mean, why wouldn't it? I'd kill my husband if he were cheating."

"Poor Ed. He hasn't got a chance if he ever decides to cheat on you," I said.

She nodded again. "You better believe it. But I don't worry about those kinds of things. He isn't the sort of man who would do that."

"You never know," Mr. Winters said. "Sometimes the person you least suspect is the one who does it. Not that I'm talking down about your husband, of course. I know he wouldn't do anything like that. Not when he's got wonderful you at home."

Lucy chuckled. "Oh now, you're just trying to flatter me."

He shrugged. "You never know when I might need to call in a favor."

"This is all very interesting," I said. "I wonder who knew about their affair. Besides your source, I mean. And I wonder if he wanted to leave his wife for Jeanette?" From what I'd heard about the victim's wife, I would have thought it was her having the affair, not him. But maybe he was frustrated with the way she was behaving and the changes she was making, and he decided to jump first.

"Maybe his wife was having an affair, and he started having an affair to get back at her," Lucy said as if reading my mind.

I nodded. "Maybe. You just never know what's going on behind closed doors. And I have a feeling that the closed doors of the Johnston residence probably had a lot going on."

Lucy took a sip of her coffee. "We've got to get more information. We've got to talk to more people. There's got to be something else that was going on in Jack's life that led up to his death."

"I heard something funny the other day," Mr. Winters said, looking at us pointedly. "I heard he was found sitting on a park bench with a newspaper in his hands. Was he murdered out there like that? I know that the two of you know."

I shook my head. "It looks as if he was killed someplace else and then brought there. At least, that's the idea that Alec is working with right now."

"Why on earth would they take him out there like

that? It was out past Langston Drive, wasn't it? That's what I heard."

I nodded. "It was." By now, word had gotten around about the details of the case, or at least most of them.

He shook his head. "People act strange these days. Back in the old days, if they wanted to murder somebody, they just shot them down, and that was the end. Or poisoned them. Or stabbed them. Whatever, but they didn't need the theatrics."

I chuckled. "Theatrics. I hadn't thought of it like that before, but you're right. Somebody had a flair for theatrics. But we'll get to the bottom of this sooner or later. Hopefully sooner."

We looked up as Mr. Johnston's daughter, Bella, walked into the coffee shop. She went up to the front counter, placed both hands on the top of it, and barked out her order. I couldn't quite hear exactly what she said, but it was her body language that told me she was not being terribly polite.

"Bella doesn't seem to be in a very good mood today," Lucy said, catching on to what was going on.

I shook my head. "No, she doesn't. But she just lost her father, so maybe that explains it."

CHAPTER 16

*A*s promised, I baked three dozen cinnamon rolls for the meal after the funeral service. I tried to make them extra special by adding extra cardamom and an additional swirl of icing, but there was no denying they were going to be served in hopes of cheering people up. The thought made me a little sad, but it couldn't be helped.

I put them in bakery boxes and ran them over to Margaret Johnston's house. It was just before 7:30 in the morning when I knocked on the door and waited. The next-door neighbor's dog barked when he heard me knock, but nobody came to the door. I knocked again, but there still was no answer. I glanced at my watch; I was right on time.

I waited a few more minutes before pounding on

the door. Maybe Margaret was still getting dressed. I hoped she wasn't in the shower because she probably wasn't going to hear me, and I wanted to get the cinnamon rolls to her as I promised.

A few moments later, the door swung open, and Bella stood there in her robe. Her hair was in a scraggly ponytail from the day before, and mascara was smudged beneath her eyes.

I smiled. "Good morning, Bella. I told your grandmother that I would bring cinnamon rolls for the meal after the funeral."

She nodded, her eyes shifting to the boxes in my hands. "Cinnamon rolls? Really?"

I hesitated, surprised she was giving me some attitude. "Yes, your grandmother was quite pleased with the cinnamon rolls I had baked, and she asked me to make some for the meal after the funeral. As a dessert." I suddenly felt awkward, standing there with the cinnamon rolls. She made no move to take them from me or to invite me in.

She shook her head. "I don't know what she was thinking. Why would anybody want cinnamon rolls for the meal after a funeral? They want casseroles and stuff. I swear, every funeral I've ever been to, they have a boatload of casseroles."

My mouth opened to say something, but I was so taken aback by her attitude, that I couldn't remember what it was. I finally forced myself to smile and nodded. "Yes, but there's always dessert after the casseroles, right? And this was what your grand-mother requested." If she had wanted pies or cakes, I would have made those, but she asked for the cinnamon rolls.

She rolled her eyes. "That woman doesn't know anything. You can come in and put them in the kitchen." She turned and walked away from me, leaving me standing there at the door.

I reminded myself that she was grieving and hurried inside with the three boxes. "What time is the funeral?" I asked her as I followed her into the kitchen. She poured herself a cup of coffee, and I set the boxes on the kitchen table.

"11:00. I don't know why you're here so early. My grandmother is getting dressed."

I nodded. "I thought that might be the reason for the delay in anyone coming to the door. I'm sure a lot of people will be there at the funeral."

She shrugged, sipped her black coffee, and didn't bother to offer me a cup. That was fine. I wasn't here on a social call. I was just delivering the cinnamon rolls I had promised.

I heard somebody padding down the stairs, and when I turned, I came face-to-face with Damon Reed. He was wearing a pair of pajama bottoms, but no shirt. I smiled and nodded, trying not to notice his bare chest. "Good morning, Damon. Margaret asked me to bring some cinnamon rolls, so I brought them by." I wasn't sure how many times I was going to feel the need to repeat myself, and I probably should have skedaddled out of there, but I was hoping to see Margaret for just a moment to tell her again how sorry I was. My heart went out to her on this difficult day.

"Cinnamon rolls? Good. I'm starving."

"Oh, they're for the meal after the funeral."

He flipped open the top of the box on top and looked them over. Now I was getting aggravated. Margaret wouldn't appreciate him snitching one of the cinnamon rolls. It would look lame to bring three boxes with a missing cinnamon roll.

He grabbed one and took a ginormous bite out of it, then nodded appreciatively. "This is great." His mouth was still stuffed with the roll when he said it.

I smiled. "Then I suppose you're going to the funeral, too."

He nodded. "Yeah, sure. I need to be there for Bella. Without me, she's nothing."

Bella rolled her eyes. "Whatever, Damon. You're just going for the food."

He chuckled. "That's true. I do love me some funeral food."

I wasn't sure what to make of these two and their attitudes. Bella was going to bury her father today, and she acted like she was completely put out by the prospect. But maybe that was how she handled grief. A lot of people didn't behave the way you would expect in those situations.

I heard somebody coming down the stairs again, and this time it was Margaret. She had her bathrobe on as well, and I could smell the soap coming off of her. She had just gotten out of the shower.

"Oh, Allie, I'm so sorry. I didn't intend to spend so long in the shower, but time just got away from me."

I smiled. "That's all right, Margaret. I brought the cinnamon rolls just like you asked," I said, shooting Damon a look.

She scowled. "Damon, are you eating one of those cinnamon rolls that Allie brought?"

He nodded and continued eating.

"Well, they were for the funeral! What are you thinking?"

I smiled, feeling supported. "I tried to tell him they were for the funeral."

She shook her head. "Why aren't you two getting dressed? You both need to shower and get dressed for the funeral."

"Grandma, it's not till eleven o'clock. We've got plenty of time," Bella said, rolling her eyes.

"We don't have plenty of time. We have so many things that we need to do for the funeral. Somebody's got to get there early and check on everything to make sure it's all set and ready to go. There's a guest book that needs to be signed, and we need to make sure it's put out for the guests."

Bella took a big swig of her coffee and slammed the cup down on the counter. "Honestly, Grandma, I don't know why you expect me to do everything for you. You need to handle these things. My mother needs to handle these things. But where is she? That's what I want to know, because I don't have time for all of this. I've got better things to do with my time, and I'm going to be busy right up until the time of the funeral."

She turned and stormed out of the kitchen.

Damon smirked, then chuckled, and shoved the rest of the cinnamon roll into his mouth. He wiped his hands on his pajama pants and sauntered after Bella.

Margaret reached for the kitchen counter for support, shaking her head. "I don't know what's got into that girl. This has all been so stressful on all of us."

I felt terrible for Margaret. She was on the verge of tears, and the last thing she needed was extra stress from Bella.

I moved closer to her. "Some people just don't handle grief well. Bella is young, and if this is the first person who was really close to her that has died, she's probably just beside herself." I put a hand on her shoulder and squeezed it.

She nodded and tried to pull herself together. "I know. Bella is a good girl, but sometimes she's not very nice." She looked up at me and blinked, and the tears were back. She blinked again, and they receded. "Her mother is grieving terribly too. I guess we're all just a mess these days. I wish we had been able to schedule the funeral sooner, so we would be past this point by now, but this was the earliest day we could get after coordinating with some of the other family members."

I nodded. "I hate that time between a death and the funeral. It's a grief limbo of sorts. Is there anything else that I can do for you today? Is there anything you need to be done that I can handle for the funeral?"

She smiled and shook her head. "No, Allie, but I certainly do appreciate you volunteering. It's very kind of you. And I appreciate those cinnamon rolls. I wish you would let me pay for them."

I shook my head. "Absolutely not. I made those cinnamon rolls for you and your family and your guests as a way to say I am sorry for your loss, and it wouldn't be right for me to take any money for them. I'm just sorry that you all are going through this."

She nodded. "I certainly do appreciate it. Thank you for everything."

"You're welcome." I hugged her and then excused myself and left.

I got into my car and sat in the silence for a minute, pulling myself together. I was shocked by Bella's and Damon's attitudes. Grief or not, I couldn't imagine my kids behaving that way. They had been the complete opposite when their father died. Was this what it was like in the Johnston household all the time?

CHAPTER 17

My first stop, after dropping off the cinnamon rolls to Margaret, was the county library to see if I could talk to Jeanette Hawkins. If Mr. Winters' source was correct, then she was having an affair with Jack Johnston, and I wondered what he had confided in her. I also wondered if their relationship was a harmonious one or if there had been troubles. The last person one would suspect of murder is a county librarian, but in my book, that made her a very real suspect.

I swung by the Cup and Bean and got a pumpkin spice latte first. Then I sat in the parking lot and waited for the library to open. I considered stopping by Lucy's house to see if she was up and about, but since we hadn't planned to go running, I thought she was probably sleeping in, as was her custom. She liked her sleep, so I was going to let her have it.

At 8:40, the librarians began arriving. The library was larger than one would expect in such a small town, so four of them showed up.

I took another sip of my pumpkin spice latte and waited the final twenty minutes. When the door was finally unlocked for business, I left my coffee in the car and headed in. They had a strict no food or drink policy.

"Good morning," Jeanette Hawkins called from the front desk when I stepped inside.

"Good morning, Jeanette," I said. I headed straight up to the front counter. "Jeanette, I'm afraid I've lost my library card. I don't know what I could have done with it. I've looked everywhere. Can I get another?" It was true. I hadn't seen it in ages.

She smiled and nodded. "Of course. We haven't seen you in here for a while, Allie." She began tapping on her computer keyboard.

I sighed. "I know. I've been thinking about that. I used to love the library when I was a little girl, but somehow I've gotten away from making regular trips in. I'm going to change that."

She nodded. "I know what you mean. I think if I didn't actually work here, I would probably have trouble finding the time to stop in. But you know, you can also get digital books online."

I shook my head. "No, I didn't know that. My gosh, what have I been missing out on? I'll have to take a look and see what there is online."

She continued tapping. "You can also reserve books online, so you can browse the shelves virtually and come in later to pick them up." She chuckled. "Who would've thought that would ever happen?"

I shook my head. "Certainly not me. I promise from now on, I'm going to make regular visits to the library. I need to get some more reading done. I've been baking batch after batch of cinnamon rolls these past couple of weeks, and I swear I have had no time for anything else, but I'm going to make time for this."

Her eyebrows rose. "Cinnamon rolls? My favorite."

"Oh gosh, I wish I'd have known that. I didn't plan to stop by here, but I dropped off three dozen to Margaret Johnston, and I could have brought an extra one for you if I had known."

She smiled. "Oh, that's all right. But I sure do love them."

"Do you know Margaret Johnston?"

She glanced at me and gave a quick shake of her head. "No, I know of her, but I don't actually know her."

I was sure she probably had heard a lot about Margaret from Jack if what Mr. Winters said was true and they had been having an affair. "The poor thing has just lost her son, Jack Johnston. Did you hear he was murdered?"

She turned to me now and if I wasn't mistaken, I saw hurt in her eyes. She nodded. "Yes, I heard about that. I knew Jack." When she said she knew Jack, her eyes widened, and she turned away quickly, as if she had just told a secret she meant to keep.

"Oh, did you? I didn't know him well, but with this being a small town, of course, you run into people. Were you close to Jack?" I held my breath, hoping she would tell me about him.

She bit her bottom lip and continued typing on the keyboard. I couldn't imagine why looking at my account would require that much typing, but now she was typing much faster than she had been.

She swallowed and shrugged. "I don't know. I mean, I knew him."

"It's such a shame that he was murdered as he was. I feel just terrible for his family, and anybody close to him."

She turned to me, and her eyes were beginning to tear up. "I guess you could say we were friends."

"Oh, I'm so sorry for your loss, then. It's just so awful."

She shook her head. "I don't know who would do such a horrible thing. He was a quiet, unassuming man. I can't imagine anybody going out of their way to kill him like that."

I nodded. "It's awful, isn't it? So you don't have any idea who might have wanted to kill him? I mean, since you were close, did he ever mention he was having issues with anyone?" Jeanette was a gentle soul, and I didn't want to push too hard, but I had to know.

She shook her head, biting her lower lip. "No, he never mentioned anybody he was having trouble with. He just—oh," she said, looking away.

I put my hand over her hand on the keyboard. "I'm sorry. I know this has to be very hard for you. I don't know how close your relationship was, but I'm going to assume that it was very close. Any information that you might have that could help the police is so important for them to know."

She sighed, turning back to me. "We were seeing each other. I'm not proud of it. I'd never gone out with a married man before, but he came into the library frequently and we would strike up conversations. He was so intelligent, and he had an interest in virtually everything. He was just very easy to talk to, and somehow, I fell for him." She looked at me as if begging me to understand what she was saying. And while I didn't approve of people having extramarital affairs, I could see that she was grieving his loss, perhaps as much as his family was.

I nodded. "I understand. Are you sure there's nothing he said to you that might help solve his murder?"

She sighed. "Not really. He was having money trouble, but money seemed to be an issue with him all the time. His family—oh, maybe I shouldn't say anything about his family. It's not as if I know them personally. He wanted to keep our relationship a secret, which was understandable."

"No, go on. What about his family?"

She glanced around, but there was no one close enough to overhear us. "They put a lot of pressure on him. A lot of pressure financially. His wife refused to work, and then there was his daughter. She was very needy, and she wanted things from him. Material things. But he said that she didn't seem to have much interest in him unless he was giving her money. I don't know if that was accurate, or if he just didn't have the relationship that he hoped for with his daughter, and he got his feelings hurt. He was a very sensitive man."

I nodded. "It must have made him angry that his wife refused to work. It's difficult having a relationship with someone who doesn't want to pull their weight."

She nodded. "It made him very unhappy. I guess she used to work about ten years ago, but she got fired from her job and ever since then she refused to even go out and look for a new one. They've got that expensive house, and she always insisted on a new car every year. That can get very expensive."

I was surprised at this. "She insisted on a new car every year? You're right, that is very expensive. And then when you couple that to the fact that she didn't want to work, it could be very frustrating. Why didn't he just put his foot down and tell her that if she wanted new car, she would have to work for it?"

She shrugged. "That was the way he was. He didn't like confrontation or drama in his life, so he tried not to ruffle her feathers too much. I suspect that in the past he did try to make her get a job, but she refused, and I'm pretty sure things got ugly."

This was interesting information. The more I dug around, the more I could see where Jack and his wife Merlene were struggling with their relationship. And all of those new clothes, and her change in the way she looked, cost money. Money that Jack most likely resented handing out since she didn't want to work for it.

"It had to be difficult to live like that."

She nodded. "It was."

"What about the money he inherited from his father? Couldn't he have paid for all those things with that?"

"I suppose, but the money also belonged to his mother. And he resented Merlene and his daughter for being so entitled."

I sighed. "It sounds like it was a difficult, chaotic household."

She nodded and slid the library card across the counter to me. "It was. It really was. There's your new library card. I'm glad that you stopped in."

I smiled. "Me too. You take care of yourself, Jeanette. And again, I'm sorry for your loss. The next time I bake some cinnamon rolls, I'm going to bring you some."

She brightened. "Oh, that's so sweet of you, Allie. I sure would appreciate that."

I nodded. "I'm going to go find some books."

I headed over to the mystery stacks to take a look at some new books.

I felt badly for Jeanette Hawkins. She seemed to care genuinely for Jack, and since the funeral would be in a couple of hours and she was here at work, I thought she probably would be missing it. That tore at my heart a bit, but it was probably the most respectful thing to do for the family.

CHAPTER 18

"*P*oor Jeanette."

I nodded as we ran along Rose Street. We had chosen a scenic neighborhood, full of fall trees. I don't know if I've mentioned this before, but I can never get enough of the fall leaves. Okay, maybe I have. This was the perfect neighborhood to run through in the fall. The scarlet oak, sugar maple, and flowering dogwood trees made for beautiful scenery. I made a mental note to look into planting a lot more trees around our house. We had plenty of them now, but planting more would not only give us more privacy but would also make me giddy with excitement every fall.

"I feel bad for her," I agreed. "I'll never condone

extra-marital affairs, but I do feel for her. She genuinely seemed to care for Jack."

She nodded, breathing heavily as we ran up an incline. "When you start messing around, you're bound to get yourself in trouble. But Jeanette Hawkins has always struck me as a nice woman, so I agree with you. I feel bad for her."

The day was sunny and pleasantly warm. A light breeze blew, but the weatherman had promised stronger winds by evening. That was fine by me. We could build a fire in the fireplace, drink cocoa, and perhaps indulge in a cinnamon roll or two. I hadn't received any new orders for them in the last couple of days, but that didn't mean I couldn't bake them for my family and myself. Besides, I had promised Jeanette that I would bring her some. Since I was going to deliver them to her workplace, I would probably have to bring extras for the other librarians and the folks who worked there. It's good to keep librarians on your side. That way, when a popular book had a lengthy waiting list and I wanted to read it, maybe they would bump me up to the top of the list. A girl can dream, right?

"I bought some new fall candles and placed them on my fireplace mantel, along with some small pumpkins that Alec and I bought from the co-op last week.

I love burning candles in the fall and winter. It feels so cozy."

She glanced at me. "I brought four new candles into the house, and Ed hasn't even noticed. I placed them on my fireplace mantel too, and I even lit them last night. He didn't say a word. Not one peep."

"Maybe he's getting senile in his old age," I suggested. "In that case, you can buy all the candles you want, and he'll never say a word."

She chuckled. "We can only hope. I need more pumpkins, though. Lots and lots of pumpkins. I wasn't impressed by the ones at the grocery store when I went the other day, so I'm going to have to stop by the co-op and see what they've got."

I nodded. "I still have to bring some fresh jams and jellies to place on my shelf. And I promised myself I was going to make some pumpkin butter. I've got to get that done." My to-do list was a mile long.

We ran along, making plans for fall, when I spotted somebody I knew up ahead.

"Look." I nodded in that direction.

Lucy grinned and glanced at me. "Lynn Johnston."

I nodded. "I'd had my doubts about her because she seemed bitter about not getting more of her father's money. Alec doesn't seem to think she makes a very good suspect. But I think anyone greedy makes a good suspect."

"Me too. You've got to watch out for those money-hungry folks. They'll kill somebody in a minute if it means they can get their hands on some money."

I chuckled. "You're telling me."

Lynn was up ahead, raking leaves in her yard. I hadn't realized that she lived on this street, but we might as well stop by and say hello since we were here.

As we got closer, we slowed our pace, and she turned to look at us and smiled.

"Good morning, Allie, good morning, Lucy. It's a beautiful day, isn't it?"

We came to a stop near her mailbox and nodded. Her yard was perfectly green, even though it was fall —one of those manicured lawns with no fence around it. "It's a perfect day for a fall run. It hasn't gotten cold yet, and it isn't too warm. As a bonus, we get to look at all the beautiful trees."

She glanced up at the big scarlet oak tree in her front yard and made a face. "Well, the trees certainly are beautiful this time of year, but I don't like raking up after them. I'm hoping if I can stay on top of the few leaves that are dropping now, it won't be so bad when the trees drop all the rest of their leaves."

"It is quite a job, keeping the leaves out of your yard," Lucy agreed. "I have Ed for that. At least, I tell him that's what I keep him around for, but he doesn't believe me."

She chuckled. "Yes, husbands tend to not like doing some of the household chores. I've been divorced for twenty years, and I don't regret it for a minute. My husband didn't just avoid household chores; he didn't want to go to work to earn his keep either. I can take care of myself better than he could."

I nodded. "Sometimes it's easier handling things on your own."

She nodded and leaned on her rake. "My brother's funeral was yesterday. It was nice. My mother pointed out the cinnamon rolls that you donated. That was really sweet of you. They were delicious. Thank you."

I nodded. "I was happy to do it. I'm glad that y'all enjoyed them."

"We had a lot of people there at the funeral," she said. "Honestly, it was more than I had imagined. Although there were a few people there that I wish hadn't bothered to show up." She made a face and kicked at a large leaf lying by her feet.

"Oh?" Lucy said. "There wasn't any trouble, was there?"

I wondered if she was talking about Jeanette Hawkins. Maybe she had gotten away from the library long enough to go to the funeral.

She smiled and shook her head. "No, there wasn't any trouble. It was just a smart-aleck kid who should have had a little more respect for her father. I'm talking about Bella and her boyfriend. I swear, I don't know why Jack didn't take control of that child when she was younger and he was capable of doing it. But she's a spoiled, spoiled girl, and she acted like she was put out to even be there at the funeral."

"I'm sorry to hear that," I said. "And I don't mean to be forward, but when I dropped the cinnamon rolls off at your mother's yesterday, I was surprised at Bella's attitude. You're right. She acted like she was put out that she had to go to the funeral."

She nodded. "Exactly. That was her attitude when she was there. You would have thought that at least for her mother and grandmother, she would have been more respectful, but no. Not her. She only thinks about herself."

"Does she stay with your mother frequently?" I asked. "And her boyfriend, too?"

She smirked. "That's more of a recent thing. She moved out of her parents' house about two months ago, and into my mother's. I keep telling my mother she needs to kick them out. They don't help her with anything around the house, and they certainly aren't paying rent."

"Oh, that's a shame," Lucy said. "It sounds like they're taking advantage of her."

She nodded. "That's exactly what's happening."

"Why did she move out of her parents' house?" I asked.

She shook her head, smiling. "She didn't exactly move out. I mean, I guess she moved out and took her things with her, but not because it was her idea. Jack kicked her out."

I was surprised to hear this. "Really?"

She nodded. "I told Jack that it was far too late in that child's life to suddenly try to tell her what to do. She's an adult, for goodness' sake. He should have kicked her out as soon as she turned eighteen and said she wasn't going to get a job. But of course, he waited." She rolled her eyes. "Again, he waited. I don't know what was wrong with that man and why he was willing to put up with so much from that girl. Of course, it was his wife's fault because she's the one who spoiled her, and she's the one who kept Jack from making her take responsibility for anything." She shrugged. "Kicking her out was a good thing, and it needed to be done. But it's made my mother's life so much harder."

"What did Merlene say about it when he kicked her out?" I asked.

"Oh, she was livid. But he did it while she was

gone on a trip, which was a smart thing to do. When she got home, they went round and round about it."

"Did Jack say anything to Bella about moving into her grandmother's house?" I couldn't imagine he would have been happy about that if he didn't even want her in his own house.

She nodded. "Yes, he told her that she needed to get out and find someplace else to live. Especially since she moved her boyfriend in with her. At least that was one thing she wouldn't dare to have done at her own house. But my poor mother, she's a soft touch just like Jack was, and she couldn't kick the girl out."

"It sounds like a mess," Lucy said. "Doesn't her mother say anything about it? Isn't she upset that she's treating her grandmother that way?"

She rolled her eyes. "Merlene? No. Merlene has always been all about herself, especially in the past several years. She spends money like it's nothing, and it's always spent on herself or Bella. I don't think she cares one way or another if Bella is sponging off of her grandmother now, as well as allowing her boyfriend to do it. I was thinking I would have to have my mother move in with me just to get her out of that house and then maybe we could sell the house, but I don't know if she'll do it. Otherwise, I don't know how we're going to get rid of Bella and that boyfriend of hers."

"That's awful," Lucy said. "I would think that her mother would be more concerned about what she was doing to her grandmother than she is."

Lynn nodded. "Me too. I guess we'll figure something out. Well, it's been nice visiting with you ladies. I've got to finish cleaning this yard, and then I've got a dentist appointment." She made a face. "I hate going to the dentist."

"Me too," I said. "It's been nice talking to you, Lynn. We'll see you around."

Lucy and I continued to run up the street, and when we were far enough out of earshot, Lucy turned to me. "That Bella sure is difficult, isn't she?"

I nodded. "She sure is. And she's selfish, and I bet she didn't like being kicked out of her house by her father."

CHAPTER 19

A large round drop of rain landed on my nose, and I looked up at the dark sky. The weatherman had been forecasting rain for several days, but we had been dry until now. I slammed my car door and hurried to the entrance of the co-op, grabbed a shopping cart, and rushed back with it.

I parked it next to my trunk to unload the precious cargo: pumpkin butter, apple butter, cranberry chutney, and apple preserves. I had said that I was going to make a fresh batch of goodies to bring down here to stock my shelves, and I finally got around to doing it. I also brought along some jam—plum, strawberry, and peach—that I had canned in the summer. There was something about canning jams, jellies, and butters that made me happy. But this time of year it was the pumpkin butter that made me smile. I used lots of cinnamon, cloves, and ginger, among other spices, to make it sweet and tasty, just the way I liked it.

"Look at that. We're going to get rain," Alec said, gazing up at the sky.

"We're going to get soaked."

He nodded. "We'll live."

I had tossed and turned all night with thoughts of everything I had learned about Jack Johnston's death running through my mind. I knew who killed him. I knew exactly who it was.

Alec loaded the jars into the shopping cart and slammed the trunk just as the dark sky opened up and pelted rain on our cozy little town. I pulled up the collar of my light windbreaker and pushed the shopping cart back to the co-op as fast as I dared. I wasn't wearing rain boots, and I didn't want to slip on the asphalt, but I also didn't want to get soaked. This would teach me not to listen to the weatherman. He may not have been accurate the previous few days, but today, he was more than making up for it.

I pushed the cart through the co-op doors and headed to my shelves. I brought along a feather duster and a damp cloth to make sure none of the jars were sticky. I had already cleaned them at home, but I liked to go over them again before putting them on the shelf for my customers.

I flipped my red curly hair over my shoulder and shook off the rain.

"Looks like we're getting a downpour," Alec said, looking at the co-op door.

I nodded, glancing around. "I hope it stops before morning. I love going for a run after it rains."

"Allie," a familiar voice rang out from behind me.

I looked over my shoulder, and Bella Johnston was headed toward us with a shopping cart of her own.

I smiled. "Good afternoon, Bella. Did you see that the rain has started? We've been expecting it for days now, and it's finally here."

She looked toward the front door and nodded. "It looks like we're about to get a downpour." She glanced at Alec but didn't acknowledge him and parked her shopping cart next to mine. It was filled with an assortment of dry goods items.

"Are you doing some shopping?" I asked.

She shook her head. "No, apparently some customers don't know where to put the items they've changed their minds about. I went around the store gathering them up. Now I'm putting them back where they belong."

I chuckled. "I bet that happens all the time."

She nodded. "It sure does." She reached into her

shopping cart and plucked out one of my jars of strawberry jam and handed it to me. "I found this over near the dry beans."

I chuckled again. "Well, I guess if it's a choice between dry beans and my strawberry jam, we know which one wins." Alec had his eye on her but didn't say anything.

She nodded. "They must have been out of their minds. I'd take strawberry jam over dry beans any day."

I nodded. "Me too." I ran my damp cloth over the jar just to be sure it was clean and set it back on the shelf. "Thanks for returning it."

"No problem. It's what I get paid for."

Alec watched her intently as we spoke. She wasn't unaware of it; she kept glancing at him, and she looked decidedly uncomfortable.

"It looks like you brought a lot of yummy things."

I nodded. "Pumpkin butter is by far my favorite, but there's also apple butter, cranberry chutney, and apple preserves. I hope you're going to pick up a jar or two."

She nodded. "I'll do that. My grandmother will love it."

I glanced at Bella. She hadn't asked me any questions, but I felt as if she wanted to know something. "How did the funeral go the other day?"

She took a deep breath and then sighed. "It was fine. It was nice. Lots of people showed up, and I know that made my mom and grandma feel good."

I nodded. "It's comforting to know that your loved one had people who cared about them."

Her eyes went to Alec. "I haven't talked to you for several days. Have you made an arrest yet?" She avoided using his name.

He shook his head. "No, not yet. I'm working on it."

Then I spotted a pretty ring on her right ring finger. It was yellow gold with a tiny pink stone. "Oh gosh, isn't that ring pretty? I love the pink and gold together."

She looked down at her hand on the shopping cart handle and frowned. "Yeah, my dad gave it to me for my sixteenth birthday. My mom wanted me to wear it to the funeral, so I did, and I just haven't taken it off yet."

I smiled at the sweetness of the gesture. "Your father had lovely taste in jewelry."

Her mouth made a straight line. "He was a cheapskate. Look how tiny the stone is. The least he could have done was get me a diamond."

I was taken aback by her attitude once again. Bella could flip-flop between sweet and agreeable and unkind in an instant.

I shook my head. "I think that ring is perfect just the way it is."

"Parents enjoy it when their children appreciate their gifts," Alec said.

She rolled her eyes. "Yeah, I guess. But he was always that way. I'd ask him for a certain thing, and he'd get me something else. Like this. I wanted a diamond ring, and this is what I got instead. He said it went with my personality." She rolled her eyes. "I don't know what he was thinking."

"That you were small and cheap?" Alec asked.

I almost dropped the jars of jam in my hands.

She glowered at him. "How dare you?"

He shrugged. "It was easy."

"Bella, did you have a good relationship with your father?" I asked in an attempt to bring down the tension.

She seemed unsure of herself for a moment. "Everybody says how wonderful my father was, but I wouldn't know about that. I never saw him. He was always too busy working or doing something he wanted to do that didn't include me. He didn't like spending time with me."

"I'm sorry," I said. "I know it can be difficult for parents to balance kids and their careers, but they usually manage to do it somehow."

She shook her head. "It wouldn't have mattered.

Even if he had been unemployed, he never would have spent any time with me. He didn't even like me. I think he wanted a boy." She glanced at Alec. What he said had thrown her off.

"Oh, Bella, I know it may have felt that way at times, but believe me, when you're a parent, you love your children. It's this innate sense inside that you need to protect them and take care of them at all costs. Even if that means working extra hours or extra jobs, you do it because you want the best for them."

She sighed. "You can think that if you want, but that isn't how my father was. He didn't want anything to do with me. And I'm supposed to be grieving his death? Why? I don't see any reason to grieve his death."

"So you didn't care about your father at all?" Alec asked.

She snorted. "No. Why would I? He always criticized me. He said I was a mistake." Her voice was cold and hard, without even a hint of emotion.

"But you had to have some feelings for him," Alec cajoled.

She shook her head and smiled a wicked smile. "I don't have any feelings for him. Honestly, I wish we had done a DNA test to see if he was even my father. I highly doubt it."

My eyes cut to Alec. "I think you get your eyes from him," I pointed out.

She shrugged. "Whatever. But I didn't cry at his funeral, and I'm not going to cry for him ever."

"There are many people who wouldn't cry about their parent dying," Alec said as he leaned on the shopping cart. "Why is it that you hate your father so much?"

She glared at him. "I told you. He couldn't stand me, and he resented me for existing. He never got me the things I wanted. It was all about him, even when he inherited that money from my grandfather. He could have bought me something with it."

"It's a shame when you don't get what you want," he said.

She pressed her lips together. She wasn't going to get the sympathy she was looking for from Alec. "He got what he deserved. I don't know who killed him, but he got what he deserved." Her hands gripped the handles of her shopping cart. The conversation had shifted from friendly and conversational to angry, and it was all downhill from there.

"Are you sure you don't know who killed him?" Alec asked. "Because I heard that you had no love for him and were angry at him. You've just confirmed what I've heard. It would be convenient for you, wouldn't it? If he suddenly died? Because then you would inherit his wealth."

I glanced at Alec. He was intense now.

She laughed. "Sure, it would have been great if he died, and then he did." She shrugged. "Oh well, a happy ending for all."

Alec didn't budge. "Maybe we should have another talk. I feel like I still have some unanswered questions."

She blinked. "Why? I don't have anything else to say."

"You don't? Because you've had a lot to say right here. How about we go downtown and talk for a few minutes?"

"I can't. I'm working." She began to push her shopping cart away, but Alec reached out and took hold of it.

"I am sure your boss would understand that you need to go downtown for a few minutes."

She glared at him and tried to push the cart, but Alec had a firm grip on it. "Fine. I'll go downtown, and I'll talk to you. But there's nothing else for me to say." She shoved the shopping cart, almost knocking it over on its side, and strode toward the entrance of the co-op. Alec was gone without a glance over his shoulder. I sighed as I watched him go. I was going to have to call Lucy to get a ride home.

CHAPTER 20

I waited around for Alec to come home. I suppose it shouldn't have come as a surprise that Bella killed her father. Not once I understood just how much disdain she held for him. We knew that going into the co-op. I had held the slightest of hopes that she hadn't done it, but I knew the truth. It was sad. Raising a child who had no regard for you as a parent must have been difficult. Worse, of course, was the fact that she betrayed her father and killed him.

It was the middle of the night when Alec finally came home. He looked tired as he removed his raincoat and hung it in the hall closet. The rain hadn't let up, and Lucy and I weren't going to be able to go running later.

"Hey," I said, going to him and wrapping my arms around him. "How are you?"

He smiled, looking down into my face. "I'm exceptional. How about you?"

I gently slapped his chest. "Stop it. You look exhausted."

He nodded. "I am exhausted."

"I can make us some hot cocoa."

He shook his head. "I think I'm going to go straight to bed. I should take a shower, but I'm not going to be able to stay awake that long."

I nodded. "You're going to tell me what happened before you fall asleep, aren't you?"

He nodded. "Of course I am." He put his arm around me, and we headed up the stairs to the bedroom with Dixie following behind us.

He sat on the edge of the bed and began taking his shoes off.

"Bella Johnston is one of the most entitled young women that I have ever met in my life. She demanded a lot from her father, and he usually delivered. But he finally got tired of delivering and demanded that she move out of the house when she refused to look for a job or go to college."

"Sometimes when you spoil a child, they never grow out of the thought that their parents are there to serve them," I sighed and looked up. Jennifer was standing in the doorway.

"I need the details," she said, leaning on the door frame, her pink robe wrapped around her.

I smiled, shaking my head. "He's just begun explaining what happened."

"As I was telling your mother, Bella was entitled, and when Jack stood up to her, she killed him."

"But why on earth was he out there in the middle of nowhere like that with his newspaper?" She crossed her arms in front of herself.

That was one thing that I couldn't understand. What was he doing out there?

He sighed as he reached out to scratch Dixie's head when he rubbed up against his leg. "It seems he used to go to the municipal park across from where he worked early in the morning to read his newspaper and drink his coffee before starting work. But recently he changed locations and began going out to the edge of town and sitting on a bench out there to read his newspaper and drink his coffee. You see, his girlfriend, Jeanette, would sometimes meet him out there, and they could have time together without being bothered."

I turned to look at him. "Wait a minute. Jeanette was out there the morning he was killed?"

He shook his head. "No. She had to go to Bangor

for a meeting at the main library. But he was still accustomed to going out there in the morning, so he did. Somehow, Bella had caught onto this fact, and she and Damon were lying in wait for him that morning. He was sitting there, quietly reading his newspaper with his coffee on the bench beside him when they walked up to him and shot him in the chest."

I shook my head. "How awful."

"Did anyone know about Jeanette?" Jennifer asked. "Because I would think that would have sent Bella over the edge earlier."

"His mother knew. But she wasn't going to expose her son."

I shook my head. "But why was the newspaper still in his hands? How come the bullet didn't go through it?"

He smiled tiredly. "When they approached him, he dropped his newspaper and knocked the coffee cup onto the ground. That's why there was a little dirt on it. Then, according to Bella, Damon shot him. Damon set him upright, placing the newspaper in his hands and setting his coffee cup back beside him on the bench as if he was just sitting there, reading like he always did. He thought it was funny." He gave me a look that said he thought the guy was an idiot. And he was.

I shook my head. "That's so sad. All of it. How

could she do it? And Damon pulled the trigger, not Bella?"

He nodded. "She claims that Damon did it. He's not willing to admit to it, but we know that they killed him, and they are both behind bars now."

"I can't believe anybody would do something like that," Jennifer said. "Honestly, what gets into people's heads?"

"I wish I could answer that," Alec said with a sigh. "It's all quite a mess."

"But it was Bella's plan? How did they intend to get away with it? I mean, they thought they would get away with it and go on living their lives?"

He nodded. "Yes, Bella came up with the idea. She thought that if somebody murdered her father, she would get her inheritance early, and she wouldn't have to bother about getting a job. She had only taken up the job at the co-op because her grandmother had insisted on it. Bella was worried she might get kicked out before she could get the inheritance money."

I groaned. I was glad Jack's killer had been found, but it was all so awful.

"What a shame," Jennifer said.

I looked at her. She had made herself scarce since promising to make an appointment with the guidance counselor at the college. "So what's going on with you, Jennifer? Have you made up your mind about what you want to do?"

She hesitated before answering. "I'm going to continue going to college. But I'm going to change my major. The problem is I haven't decided what I want it to be, so I'm going to finish the semester, and hopefully by then, I'll have it figured out. Sorry. That means I'm probably going to have to go an extra year or so until I can complete a new major. I'm going to find a part-time job to help pay for it."

I nodded. "I just want you to be happy with whatever you choose to do."

She nodded. "I will be."

Alec sighed. "If you two will excuse me, I've got to go to sleep. I can barely keep my eyes open."

Jennifer smiled. "No problem. I'm going down to the kitchen to get a snack, and I will leave you to your sleep."

"Good night," I said.

"Good night," she said, heading off to the kitchen.

I looked at Alec and put my arm around his waist. "I'm glad this is resolved. I hate that it was his daughter who did it, but I'm glad that the killers are behind bars."

He nodded. "Me too. I'm also kind of glad that I never had any kids."

I looked at him and chuckled. "Stop it. Your kids would never grow up to be murderers."

He kissed me. "That's right. Because I carry a gun, and they would know better."

I rolled my eyes and got up to get dressed for bed.

I would rather it had been somebody else who had killed Jack Johnston. The thought of a child killing their parent was beyond dreadful. I also felt badly for Margaret and Merlene. They had lost their daughter and granddaughter to probable life imprisonment. Not to mention their son and husband to murder.

And Jennifer? I sighed. I hoped she would get things straightened out and feel confident about the new major she would choose. I decided to have faith in her to do just that.

The End

SIGN UP

Sign up to receive my newsletter for updates on new releases and sales:

https://www.subscribepage.com/kathleen-suzette

Follow me on Facebook:

https://www.facebook.com/Kathleen-Suzette-Kate-Bell-authors-759206390932120

BOOKS BY KATHLEEN SUZETTE:

A Freshly Baked Cozy Mystery, book 8
Red, White, and Blue Murder
A Freshly Baked Cozy Mystery, book 9
Mummy Pie Murder
A Freshly Baked Cozy Mystery, book 10
Wedding Bell Blunders
A Freshly Baked Cozy Mystery, book 11
In a Jam
A Freshly Baked Cozy Mystery, book 12
Tarts and Terror
A Freshly Baked Cozy Mystery, book 13
Fall for Murder
A Freshly Baked Cozy Mystery, book 14
Web of Deceit
A Freshly Baked Cozy Mystery, book 15
Silenced Santa
A Freshly Baked Cozy Mystery, book 16
New Year, New Murder
A Freshly Baked Cozy Mystery, book 17
Murder Supreme
A Freshly Baked Cozy Mystery, book 18
Peach of a Murder
A Freshly Baked Cozy Mystery, book 19
Sweet Tea and Terror
A Freshly Baked Cozy Mystery, book 20
Die for Pie
A Freshly Baked Cozy Mystery, book 21

Gnome for Halloween
A Freshly Baked Cozy Mystery, book 22
Christmas Cake Caper
A Freshly Baked Cozy Mystery, book 23
Valentine Villainy
A Freshly Baked Cozy Mystery, book 24
Cupcakes and Beaches
A Freshly Baked Cozy Mystery, book 25
Cinnamon Roll Secrets
A Freshly Baked Cozy Mystery, book 26

A COOKIE'S CREAMERY MYSTERY

Ice Cream, You Scream
A Cookie's Creamery Mystery, book 1
Murder with a Cherry on top
A Cookie's Creamery Mystery, book 2
Murderous 4th of July
A Cookie's Creamery Mystery, book 3
Murder at the Shore
A Cookie's Creamery Mystery, book 4
Merry Murder
A Cookie's Creamery Mystery, book 5
A Scoop of Trouble
A Cookie's Creamery Mystery, book 6
Lethal Lemon Sherbet
A Cookie's Creamery Mystery, book 7

A LEMON CREEK MYSTERY

Murder at the Ranch
A Lemon Creek Mystery, book 1
The Art of Murder
A Lemon Creek Mystery, book 2
Body on the Boat
A Lemon Creek Mystery, book 3

A Rainey Daye Cozy Mystery, book 8
Fish Fry and a Murder
A Rainey Daye Cozy Mystery, book 9
Cupcakes and a Murder
A Rainey Daye Cozy Mystery, book 10
Lemon Pie and a Murder
A Rainey Daye Cozy Mystery, book 11
Pasta and a Murder
A Rainey Daye Cozy Mystery, book 12
Chocolate Cake and a Murder
A Rainey Daye Cozy Mystery, book 13
Pumpkin Spice Donuts and a Murder
A Rainey Daye Cozy Mystery, book 14
Christmas Cookies and a Murder
A Rainey Daye Cozy Mystery, book 15
Lollipops and a Murder
A Rainey Daye Cozy Mystery, book 16
Picnic and a Murder
A Rainey Daye Cozy Mystery, book 17

A PUMPKIN HOLLOW MYSTERY SERIES

Candy Coated Murder
A Pumpkin Hollow Mystery, book 1
Murderously Sweet
A Pumpkin Hollow Mystery, book 2
Chocolate Covered Murder
A Pumpkin Hollow Mystery, book 3
Death and Sweets
A Pumpkin Hollow Mystery, book 4
Sugared Demise
A Pumpkin Hollow Mystery, book 5
Confectionately Dead
A Pumpkin Hollow Mystery, book 6
Hard Candy and a Killer
A Pumpkin Hollow Mystery, book 7
Candy Kisses and a Killer

A Pumpkin Hollow Mystery, book 8
Terminal Taffy
A Pumpkin Hollow Mystery, book 9
Fudgy Fatality
A Pumpkin Hollow Mystery, book 10
Truffled Murder
A Pumpkin Hollow Mystery, book 11
Caramel Murder
A Pumpkin Hollow Mystery, book 12
Peppermint Fudge Killer
A Pumpkin Hollow Mystery, book 13
Chocolate Heart Killer
A Pumpkin Hollow Mystery, book 14
Strawberry Creams and Death
A Pumpkin Hollow Mystery, book 15
Pumpkin Spice Lies
A Pumpkin Hollow Mystery, book 16
Sweetly Dead
A Pumpkin Hollow Mystery, book 17
Deadly Valentine
A Pumpkin Hollow Mystery, book 18
Death and a Peppermint Patty
A Pumpkin Hollow Mystery, book 19
Sugar, Spice, and Murder
A Pumpkin Hollow Mystery, book 20
Candy Crushed
A Pumpkin Hollow Mystery, book 21

Trick or Treat
A Pumpkin Hollow Mystery, book 22
Frightfully Dead
A Pumpkin Hollow Mystery, book 23
Candied Murder
A Pumpkin Hollow Mystery, book 24
Christmas Calamity
A Pumpkin Hollow Mystery, book 25

Printed in Great Britain
by Amazon